THE BILLIONAIRE'S SECRET BABY

BRITISH BILLIONAIRES
BOOK THREE

DIANA FRASER

CHAPTER 1

*H*arrison Richmond and his two friends roared up to the thatched building on their motorbikes, coming to a halt in a cloud of dust. The bar was wedged between the tropical forest and a crescent of white sand, which curved like a smile around the crystal-clear azure waters of the Caribbean. A bicycle leaned against its wall and a couple of rusting cars with windows caked in dust were parked outside. A mangy dog stood barking at them, obviously annoyed at having his sleep disturbed.

"Where the hell have you brought us?" Harrison asked his friends, who'd insisted on traveling to the remote island. "Have we really endured those treacherous roads for this?"

"I was told there's a bar here," said one of his friends. He looked at the lone building sheltered by swaying palm trees. "I guess that's it." He turned to Harrison with a shrug. "What do you reckon, Frío? Might as well have one drink before we leave."

Harrison ignored the nickname, which reflected his fierce reputation on the polo fields of Argentina. Some people might have objected to being described as a cold-hearted man—*El hombre de corazón frío,* or *frío* for short. But Harrison reckoned it was a compliment and a useful warning to his competitors. He never let emotion get in the way of winning.

"Leave the island, you mean," he replied. "This place is dead."

"I was told it was beautiful."

"It may be beautiful, but there's nothing going on," said Harrison, surveying the picture-perfect scene, which stirred only anxiety in him. He liked noise. He liked variety. He liked anything which didn't leave him alone with his thoughts and feelings, although he'd never admit to those.

"Yeah, how about we don't even bother with a drink? Just get the hell off this island?" said his other friend.

Harrison was about to agree when the dog was silenced by a sharp command from inside the bar, and he heard something which robbed him of any thought. Someone was playing Chopin on a piano. And not just picking out the notes but playing it with a sensitivity which took his breath away.

Harrison pushed his sunglasses onto his head and walked around to the front of the building.

"Come on, Frío, let's go!"

Harrison held up a hand, silencing his friends. The bar's frontage was open to the elements and the chairs and tables outside were empty, save for a plastic cup, which rolled back and forward in the breeze. He sheltered his eyes and peered into the dark interior. The place was nearly empty, except for a couple of old men seated at the bar and a woman in the corner playing a small upright piano, which was missing its back. It sounded like an old saloon piano but, despite that, the effect of the music was devastating. It filled the air, reaching out to him with invisible tentacles which wrapped around him and held him firm.

"Frío?" called his friend. "Are you coming?"

He wasn't going anywhere soon. There was something about the music which got to him and he couldn't figure out why. And, until he did, he wasn't leaving. "Change of plan," he called out to his friends, who were already returning to their motor bikes. "I'm going to stay awhile. You two leave if you want."

"See you back at the hotel, then."

He heard the roar of the bikes retracing their journey back to the small, one-horse town where they were staying as he walked inside, drawn by some instinct he couldn't place. He forced himself not to stare at the pianist, whose head was bowed away from him, as if she were lost in some faraway world. A quick glance had revealed long, slender tanned arms and dark hair piled into a messy bun. She was barefoot and wearing shorts and a t-shirt. Unremarkable, and yet the magic she created with her music was anything but unremarkable.

He continued on to the bar, greeted the bartender, and ordered a beer. He turned his back to the piano so he could listen more intently to the piece, while he took a long slug of his beer. He'd heard it before. It was some kind of dreamy classical piece, except he remembered it sounding very different—not so tinny, not so jangly. He assumed it was the dilapidated state of the piano which gave it that quality. He tried to place the memory, which nudged at the edge of consciousness.

And then it hit him. Full force. He closed his eyes as the long-hidden memory, usually too painful to remember, blasted into his mind with the force of a freight train, pushing everything aside and filling him with all the vivid senses associated with the memory. It was two years ago when he'd last heard the piece of music being played. He'd been on a brief trip to the UK and had called in for a few hours to see his Aunt Beth—the person he'd felt closest to in the world. She'd wanted him to stay longer, but he'd had to get back to the US.

The summer dusk had been inching toward night and candles had flickered around his aunt as she'd concentrated on her music. She'd always been like that. Whatever she was doing, whoever she was talking to, held her full attention. It was one reason people found her so charming, so magnetic—as if they were the only one in the world in whom she was interested. But he knew it was especially true in his case. He'd been the son she'd never had, and he'd never doubted her love for him. And, as soon as the music had faded away that long ago evening in Marsh House, she'd looked up at him and smiled. He'd loved that smile. And he'd loved that woman. He'd only spent a few hours with her then because he had a plane to catch. He'd have spent longer if he had known it was to have been the last time he saw her.

He blinked as the memory receded. An islander with a weathered face wearing a sweat-stained cap shifted on his stool, and he found himself gazing directly at the pianist. Later he'd wonder if it had been partly the residue of feeling remaining after invoking Aunt Beth's memory, which made him react so strongly to this woman—this stranger, this siren who'd lured him to her with her music. Whether or not it had been, he couldn't have said, because it was soon woven tight with other emotions and the two became inseparable.

All he knew at that moment, when his gaze first locked onto hers, was that he knew her. Even as his instinct told him this, his brain refuted it. But, it seemed, for once his brain had no say in the matter and he found himself walking over to her, following that visual connection.

If the first meeting of the eyes had been one of recognition, the second had been of instant desire. She'd remained completely still. Her hands lingered on the keys of the dying notes, her eyes fixed on him. It was like someone had shot a connecting line between them and neither could look away.

He rested his glass on the piano, which bore the water marks of countless other glasses.

"That was beautiful," he said.

She withdrew her hands and gave him a brief smile.

"Thank you." She ran her fingers over the notes, in a last caress, and looked up at him once more. "Chopin probably isn't what these guys"—she glanced at the barman and the handful of regulars who sat at the bar—"would prefer to hear. But they humor me."

Of course they would humor her, Harrison thought. Who wouldn't? Her voice was a sexy mix of English and Italian, and just one look into those burnt amber eyes made you forget everything, except trying to coax that flare of warmth from them again so you could lose yourself in them. He cleared his throat.

"So," he said, grasping for something normal to say. "Is this a regular gig?"

She smiled and her face lit up. "I don't get paid, if that's what you mean. No, I'm living here at the moment, and don't have a piano of my own, so…"

"So you come here to play."

She nodded, and their gazes tangled again, and desire ratcheted up a notch. "Yes." She bit her lip and tore her gaze from his, as if determined to quash the intensity he'd seen there. She jumped up. "I… I should go now."

"Wait!" he said, not wanting her to leave. "Can I buy you a drink?" She paused and he could read the indecision in her tense shoulders. "It's the least I could do in return for that Chopin. It took me back. My aunt used to play it."

Her face relaxed, and he knew he'd said something right. Maybe it was the homely mention of his aunt which made her feel less nervous.

"You know Chopin?"

"Not personally," he said with a smile, trying desperately to win her over. It worked. She laughed. "But he was my aunt's favorite composer." Still, she didn't move. "She especially liked his preludes," he ventured, hoping he could break down the last of her reserve.

Her face lit up. "Me, too! There's a coolness and control to them, but you can hear the emotion vibrating underneath. And it's always different, depending on the player." She paused, as if she'd spoken too much and wasn't used to it.

"I didn't hear any of the coolness, only the emotion," he said.

"Maybe because of your aunt."

"Maybe," he said. "Or maybe there's more emotion than coolness *in you.*"

She grunted softly and looked away.

"How about that drink?"

He held his breath while she hesitated, weighing up unknown arguments. He'd never had to wait for an answer from a woman, nor hold his breath while he did so. The novelty of the situation appealed to his need for variety.

She nodded. "Just one, maybe."

"Just one," he agreed. He smiled. He was pretty sure one would be enough. "Champagne?" he suggested.

She frowned. He'd made a mistake. Seemed there was something about champagne she didn't like. Another difference between her and the women he usually met.

She offered him a hesitant smile. "I'd prefer a lemonade, please."

"Lemonade it is," he said, turning to the barman and ordering the drink. As the barman poured it, he was aware of the woman walking towards him. He forced himself not to look. There was something about her— something shy, like a deer alert to hunters, ready to bolt. He didn't want her to bolt. He passed her the lemonade and took a seat at the bar. He reckoned she wouldn't want to sit at a secluded beach-side table, out of view of the bar. And he didn't blame her.

"Thank you," she said, slipping onto the stool beside him.

He extended his hand. "My name's Harrison, by the way."

She accepted it and he gave it a brief, firm, business-like handshake to reassure her. There was a hint of relief in her smile.

"I'm Paris."

"Pleased to meet you, Paris," he repeated, wondering to himself what on earth a beautiful woman with a glamorous name was doing in the back of beyond. "And what brings you here, to Hermosa?"

She studied her drink a fraction too long before shrugging. "Just hanging out at the beach for a while." She gave him a shy smile. "Taking some time out. You?"

"A whim." He grinned. "I'm on the island with some friends of mine. We decided to island-hop across the Caribbean." He scrunched up his face ruefully. "I was beginning to regret it."

"Why?" she asked. "Hermosa is a beautiful island."

"Sure. But I need more than beauty to hold my interest." His eyes latched onto hers. "You can find beauty anywhere."

"So what usually holds your interest?"

He shrugged. "Honestly?" He set his beer on the table. "Variety. Different things, moving on."

"Oh!" she said, obviously surprised. Whether at his honesty, his deliberate lack of corny chat-up lines or his actual answer, he couldn't tell. "Sounds like you're running from something."

His gaze returned sharply to his drink. Maybe honesty was over-rated. Perhaps he should try a different tack. "It's also my job. I..." He hesitated a moment before deciding to go with the vague option. "I work with horses." It paid off. She gave him a more relaxed smile. "Except at the moment. I'm between jobs, hence the island-hopping. How about you? What brings you here?"

"I came here for a vacation six months ago and never left."

"Really? Don't you find it a bit on the quiet side?"

She shot him a glance, which he couldn't decipher. "I like quiet. Besides, my mother left me some money when she died, which is enough to live on."

"I'm sorry."

She raised an eyebrow in query.

"About your mother dying. My mother has passed too."

She searched his face, and he realized something more was needed to break down the last of the reserve between them. Emotion. Women liked emotion. He schooled his features into a sad expression, though he hadn't thought about his mother in years. "It was pretty devastating at the time."

Her hand reached out and gripped his. "And it never gets any easier, does it?"

He shook his head, surprised at the effect her touch had on him. He knew in that moment that he'd do anything to keep that connection. He brought his other hand to rest over hers, struck by the softness of her skin and elegance of her pianist's fingers. She was all delicacy —of limbs, bone structure and, it seemed, of spirit. 'Handle with care' was written all over her. And, if he had the chance, he most definitely would.

"But we're here now. The sun is setting, the air is warm, and the company is excellent. I propose a toast." He raised his beer bottle to her tumbler of lemonade. "To life, and the future."

"The future? I can't think that far ahead." Then she laughed. "How about to the present? To tonight?"

He clinked his bottle to her lemonade. "Tonight," he murmured, his eyes never leaving hers. He very much liked the sound of that.

CHAPTER 2

*L*ittle by little the conversation began to flow, with Paris edging closer to him, her hair brushing his bare arm, and her laugh thrilling him deep inside. The second drink was a beer, which he took to be a good sign.

He wasn't much of a talker but coaxed her into conversation. Although he couldn't have said what they were talking about because it wasn't what either of them were focused on. Desire filled her eyes, whether she was laughing at some silly anecdote he told, or giving her impression of countries they'd both visited. It didn't matter what the subject, her searching gaze communicated a different message—one of intense attraction and something else. He sensed she was trying to figure out why the connection was so strong between them. But there was no explanation that a simple glance, or occasional touch could provide. They only sparked a deeper need. A need to touch, to inhale, to taste, anything to satisfy his senses—all of which yearned for her.

The hours slipped by as easily as if they were both drifting on a swift river towards an inevitable end. It wasn't until the lights behind the bar suddenly went out that they both looked around to find the place empty. The barman shone a torch at them.

"Time to go, folks."

They looked at each other and grinned, suddenly embarrassed. "I didn't notice the time," she said.

"That went by quick," he said at the same time.

They laughed, and walked outside, followed by the barman who slid down a shutter on the bar. He pointed to Harrison's bike. "Hope you've got somewhere to stay around here. I wouldn't recommend you try to use the road in the dark, not unless you're familiar with it."

"It'll be fine," Harrison said automatically.

"No, really," Paris said. "That road is incredibly dangerous. I should have thought to tell you, but I kind of got side-tracked."

Her face was lit only by the stars. The pale silver light glanced off her cheekbones and lingered on her open lips.

"We both got side-tracked," he said.

They were alone now, and neither seemed willing to move or to speak to break the spell. The quiet of the night was accentuated by the sound of the sea rushing up the steep beach as if it wanted to consume it, before dragging back again, defeated. Before he could stop himself, he reached out and took her hand. Whether to shake it, kiss it, or pull her closer to him, he couldn't have said. He simply needed to touch her. She didn't withdraw her hand.

"I've had a lovely evening," he said.

"Me too. It was unexpected."

"Very unexpected. You know, from the moment I heard the piano, I knew something remarkable was about to happen."

She huffed a short laugh. "Remarkable? Like what exactly?"

"Like *you* exactly."

Her face fell into a serious expression. "I'm not remarkable. I'm really not. I'm ordinary."

He shook his head. "Whatever you want to believe, I'm sorry, but you are the opposite to ordinary." She'd somehow moved a little closer now. "May I kiss you?"

She nodded, her lips parted in invitation. He bridged the gap between them and tentatively pressed his lips to hers. He wasn't prepared for what happened next. A short sharp shock slammed into him, and she gasped as if she, too, felt the same impact of intense desire. The kiss deepened immediately, with his lips searching hers and their tongues tangling with a deep-rooted passion which had been simmering all night and which had now had been ignited by the kiss.

He put his arms around her, and his hands explored her shoulders, before slipping to the hollow of her back. She leaned into him and didn't back off when his erection pressed against her stomach. Instead, she gasped against his mouth and slid her hands around him, before lowering them until they curved under his butt. He needed no more invitation and pulled her tight against him. She tasted of lemons and honey and he wanted to lose himself in her. Eventually, he pulled away.

"Paris, I should leave before I can't."

"It's too late for that," she said, her voice sexy-husky.

"It's too dangerous to drive the mountain pass at night. I have a spare bed."

His hopes plummeted. He'd have preferred the same bed, but at least he'd spend the night with her. "Thank you, that would be great."

"This way," she said, leading him up a darkened track. The narrow path was like a forgotten tunnel beneath the palm trees. For once in his life, he had no idea where he was going and he didn't care. At that moment, he'd follow her anywhere. Eventually they emerged at a small house which stood on its own, with only the beach in front of it.

"Would you like a drink?"

"Great, thanks." He thought he'd pretty much agree to anything she said.

"Take a seat." She indicated a wooden bench over-looking the beach. "I'll bring them out."

He wondered if she regretted offering him a bed for the night, whether she thought sitting outside would be safer. He did as she suggested and looked out at the empty dark sea, flecked with white, star-topped waves. The constant flop of the waves onto the sand and drag as it pulled the sand back into its depth would have been soporific if his whole being wasn't focused on a woman he'd never been more desperate to make love to.

"Here," she said, interrupting his reverie. "Hope it's okay. It's all I have." He took a swig from the bottle and tried hard to stop a grimace. "Um, lemonade," he said. "It's a while since I tasted this."

Her laughter filled the air, and she sat down next to him. But not too close, he noticed. It seemed she wanted a little distance between them. Then the laughter faded.

"And it's been a while since I've talked with anyone from outside the island."

"You don't miss the outside world?"

"I *didn't*."

"But you do now?"

"I think so."

"Tell me, Paris, why do you stay here, alone?"

She shrugged. "I feel safe."

"Really? It's pretty remote. Surely you'd feel safer in the city? With locks and doors to hide behind."

"The bartender doesn't live far away, and no one comes here." He could just discern her frown in the dim light. "Besides, in the city, anyone can find you. But no one knows I'm here."

"Not even your family?"

Her face stiffened. "*Especially* not my family."

"Hm," he said thoughtfully, realizing he'd struck the reason she was keeping a low profile on this remote island. "Families can be tricky."

"Your family is in England somewhere, judging by your accent?"

He nodded. "My eldest brother lives in the family home in Norfolk. He's about to have his first child."

She paused a moment. "Do you have a family? Wife and children?"

"God no! I don't want children."

"Oh," she said, surprised. "So, do you get back to see your brother often?"

"Only if we're both in London or overseas at the same time. I don't go to Norfolk." He shuddered. "Nothing against Sebastian, but Norfolk doesn't hold pleasant memories for me. I travel the world and am happy to go anywhere except Norfolk. That's the last place in the world I ever want to go."

She looked away again and was silent. He leaned over and touched her arm. She turned immediately to him.

"You look miles away."

"I was thinking that we have so many things in common, including our lack of contact with our families. I sensed a connection with you when I first saw you."

"I felt it too."

"And then there's also the fact that we prefer to keep a low profile, prefer a quiet life."

He sucked his teeth, unwilling to break this string of commonalities to admit that he lived his life in the spotlight and that this evening was something very different for him. But her expression silenced him. Her eyes were dark pools into which he wanted to sink. He knew he'd find bliss there.

"So many things," he said vaguely, "I wonder what else?"

He refused to reach out to her, despite an aching need to touch her. She had to make the first move. The blackness of the night all around them seemed to pulse with tension, wound tighter by the squawk of a nocturnal bird finding its prey, before the silence sunk back into a something more on edge, expectant.

Suddenly, she jumped up and paced away from him. Then she pivoted and walked up to him. He stayed stock still. She placed her hands on his shoulders and gripped them. The whites of her eyes were bright against her hair, which was a shade darker than the indigo-black of the star-studded sky. Although he sensed her need was as strong as his own, he wasn't prepared for what happened next.

She pressed her mouth to his, with a strength of passion which literally took his breath away. Her fingers pressed into his flesh as if she wanted to impress herself into him in every way. Her tongue found his in a hot, panting swirl of desire.

The next moment she sat astride him, her sex pressing against his erection as she wriggled closer, the palms of her hands cupping his cheeks as the kiss deepened, and her breathing changed to urgent panting.

With one swift movement, he stood up, his hands firmly keeping her butt and legs in place around his hips. Then she pulled away, slid to standing and fumbled with his zipper. He pressed his hand over hers.

"Do you have any protection here?"

She pressed her forehead against his and rocked against him. Her breath was hot on his cheek and he felt as if he were on fire.

"No. None."

"Me neither. I wasn't expecting the evening to end like this." He grimaced and pulled her hand away.

"No," she said, placing her hand over his erection, fondling it from the outside of his jeans, before flicking open the top button. "I don't care."

"You should care," he said, but he could no more stop her from yanking down his zipper than fly. He groaned as she took him in both hands and caressed him. Then she suddenly stepped away, pulled off her t-shirt and tossed it on the bench. She wasn't wearing a bra—something he'd noticed when he'd first seen her. But before he could reach out and caress her breasts, she'd unzipped her shorts and stepped out of both them and her knickers. They landed on top of her t-shirt. She stood in front of him, completely naked, and he thought he'd died and gone to heaven.

She stepped toward him, linked her arms around his neck, and kissed him deeply. He moaned as his hands wandered over her bare, silky skin before finding the slick place between her legs. It was her turn to moan. She moved her hips against his until he couldn't stand it any longer and picked her up. Her legs wrapped around his hips, and they continued to kiss as he carried her inside. It was dark in the one-room hut, but enough starlight streamed in through the open window for him to spot the bed. He lay her on it and began to explore her body with his lips and mouth and tongue.

As his tongue found its target, her breathing became more rapid. She threaded her fingers through his hair and bucked her hips against his face. Suddenly, she cried out into the tropical night. Another successful nocturnal hunt.

He lay down beside her. He'd thought this would be enough, given their lack of protection, but it wasn't. And her breath was hot on his body, her tongue wicked against his sensitive skin. And her sex, as she pushed him onto his back and held herself above his throbbing erection, wet against his tip. And he knew in that moment that caution had just been thrown out the window. She slid onto him, sinking over him, taking every last inch of him inside of her. She stayed there for a moment, and then she quickened her pace as she sensed his own response intensify. Faster and faster she moved, until she cried out at the same time he came. She arched her back as she ground down on him, keeping him buried deep inside of her for one long moment before she collapsed into his arms.

MUCH LATER, as the first signs of dawn penetrated the beach house, Harrison thought with a satisfied smile, that he didn't want to leave her. She lay fast asleep in his arms, her hair spilled over his chest. Tenderly, he kissed the top of her head. The first time they'd made love it had been through sheer need but, afterwards, it had all been about discovering each other and pleasuring each other—slowly, sensuously and tenderly. He'd never known a night like it.

His phone suddenly dinged, and he groped for it quickly, not wanting to disturb her. He frowned at the screen, re-read the message in disbelief, and then groaned. It seemed even here he couldn't escape the paparazzi. Someone must have tipped them off and he, in turn, had been tipped off. They were on their way there now. He winced at the memory of her clothes scattered outside the cottage. He had to clear things up before they arrived.

He eased himself from under her. She blinked and reached out for him, but he rose and walked toward the door. They didn't have much time.

"Where are you going?" she asked in a tone which made him want to return straight back to bed.

He grimaced and pushed his fingers through his hair, ignoring the very clear need of his body. "To tidy up."

"Tidy up?"

"Yep. Your clothes are outside the house."

"So? There's no one to see them."

"There will be soon, I'm afraid."

She frowned and sat up. His eyes dropped to her breasts, their nipples hard and ready for his mouth. He forced himself to concentrate. She valued privacy and knew she wouldn't be impressed with what was about to happen.

"What are you talking about? No one ever comes here."

"Until now."

"No they won't. Why would they?"

"Because I'm here."

"What do they want with you? And, besides, who are *they*?"

"*They* are paparazzi, and they want to fill their quota, I should imagine, of gossip columns," he added.

"But why would they want to gossip about you?"

"Ah," he grinned ruefully, raking his fingers through his hair. "I might have forgotten to tell you I play polo."

"Polo?"

"Yes, I guess I'm well known."

"How well known?"

"Sort of…" He winced. "Famous."

Her face paled instantly and her eyes changed from heated desire to stone cold anger. "And yet you didn't tell me."

He shrugged. "I didn't reckon you needed to be bothered with my problems."

"Only if they might become my problems, too."

"Why would they?" he asked.

But she didn't answer. Instead, she jumped out of bed, walked around gathering his things and thrust them into his arms. "Here you are. You'd better go."

"Sure. But I'll be back. I'll collect my gear from the hotel and then I'll be back." He tipped up her chin. "Okay?"

The sound of cars arriving at the bar and car doors being slammed drifted down to the beach house. There was no chance of retrieving his motorbike and escaping their probing lenses anymore.

"Quickly, get dressed." He tossed her the clothes he'd collected from the bench outside the house. "Stay inside, and I'll deal with this. I'll get this lot off my back and then come back here for you. Don't go anywhere," he said, momentarily arrested by the sight of her standing naked, holding onto her clothes, her eyes fierce. "Don't go anywhere," he said with a smile, before disappearing into the melee of people who'd swarmed up the path and were now snapping photos of him. He'd suck it up, for her. But he'd be back as soon as he could.

LATER IN THE DAY, after the paparazzi had been paid off with exclusive photos and an interview, Harrison returned to the isolated bay and Paris's beach house. He couldn't wait to see her again. But, as he arrived at the bay in a car this time, he knew something was different as soon as he drew up outside the house. The shutters were closed. *Everything* was closed. And there was no sign of either her car or the wind chimes which had been hanging outside the house. No sign of her at all. Fear gripped his gut as he got out, slammed the car door in the dusty heat of the afternoon, and walked over to the house. To his relief, the door was open, but when he entered, he realized why. There was nothing inside to steal. *Nothing.*

Not a trace of the woman who'd changed everything for him—the woman he'd have stayed in one place for. The place was empty—as empty as he felt.

CHAPTER 3

Five months later...

"Pregnant?" Harrison said, half-whisper, half-groan. He clenched the phone as he listened to his private investigator give him proof that the woman he'd be tracking for the last five months was, indeed, pregnant with his child. It couldn't be anyone else's. According to his PI, Paris Knight, or Caparelli—her real name—kept herself very much to herself. And there'd been no trace of any men either before or after him. Up until now Harrison had only wanted to know who she was, and where she was—this woman who he couldn't forget. But not anymore. Her pregnancy changed everything.

"And her address?" He frowned when he heard the answer. "What do you mean you don't know? She must have realized you were following her, you idiot!" He closed his eyes at the PI's excuses. "Just find her!"

Harrison finished the call and thrust his phone back in

the pocket of his tux. He sucked in a sharp breath, as he fought to control the strange mixture of frustration and need which filled him every time he thought about Paris —which was practically all the time.

He released his breath with a grunt and tilted his head to look up at the wooden beams of the converted barn from which an enormous crystal chandelier hung, lights twinkling in the lofty shadows. The frustration and need were replaced by a sadness which had been his constant companion since the day she'd left him. Where was she?

A hand on his shoulder interrupted his thoughts.

"Hey, Harrison!" He turned to find Lily, his brother Alexander's new wife, with a challenging look on her beautiful face. He forced himself back into the moment and smiled. Who wouldn't when confronted with the beautiful, outrageous Lily McGuire—as of today, Lily Richmond? She was still wearing her wedding dress, although it was gone mid-night, and she'd spent the evening dancing. Apparently, most brides changed for the party, but not Lily. The outrageously sexy, bright red dress, which fitted her voluptuous figure so snugly, continued to ensure she was the focus of the evening. Although she'd been persuaded to unclip the flamboyant train after she'd got her stiletto heel caught in it. The vicar hadn't known where to look when she'd walked up the aisle of the centuries-old church across the road from their new home—a converted barn in Essex which apparently Lily had loved for years. And, after a few meetings, he and his elder brother Sebastian almost forgot how sexy she was because of her other plentiful attributes—her bright mind and forthright personality. You didn't mess with Lily Richmond.

"Hey, Lily!" he responded.

"Why the long face?"

"Must be woman trouble," said Alexander, slipping a hand around Lily's waist. "It's the only kind us Richmond men have."

"What do you mean?" asked Lily indignantly, pivoting in Alexander's embrace so she was face-to-face with him.

"Exactly what I say," murmured Alexander, kissing his wife until she forgot what she'd been so riled about in the first place. Harrison slipped away, not wanting any further interrogation from his new sister-in-law, or to see how loved-up they were. He was pleased for them. He really was. But the happiness his two brothers had found in their new wives only emphasized his own stupidity— he'd allowed the woman who haunted his dreams to slip through his fingers.

But Harrison got no further than the door before he felt a more gentle hand on his arm.

"Harrison?" He glanced around to find Sebastian's wife, Indra, looking up at him with concerned dark eyes. "Are you all right? I couldn't help overhearing your phone conversation back there."

"Sure. I'm just trying to sort something out."

She tilted her head to one side in query. He doubted anything would get past her. "Sounded pretty important."

He pressed his lips together, scared he might inadvertently reveal the swirling chaos of confusion which was all he had in place of what other people called their feelings.

"Yep," he said shortly. "But not as important," he said, giving her a brotherly hug, "as my niece." He glanced down at her very pregnant stomach. "Any sign she's going to put in an appearance soon?"

She grimaced. "I hope so. I'm a week overdue already. I'm booked in at Norwich Hospital to be induced next week."

Harrison didn't know what being 'induced' entailed, and he certainly didn't wish to know. But from the glances his big brother, Sebastian, was throwing their way, it was clear he was concerned.

"It'll be fine, I'm sure. Sebastian will look after you." He offered his arm with a flourish of old-fashioned courtesy. "Let me take you back to him before he comes over and claims you."

Indra frowned. "Okay, but when you're ready to tell me what the matter is, you know I'm here for you."

"I do," he said. "And thanks." Apparently reassured, they joined Sebastian, Alexander and Lily. He appreciated her kindness, but knew there was no way on God's earth he was going to tell his sweet sister-in-law—or anyone come to that—about his obsession with a bare-foot pianist who responded to his every touch, every look, every thrust with a flare of heat in those hypnotic amber eyes.

As he returned to the small group that was all that was left of the wedding party, he couldn't help envy his brothers for finding such amazing women—Lily, who had to be one of the sexiest women he'd ever met and Indra, who had to be the sweetest. Harrison wondered if he'd ever find the same happiness. Judging by the way things were going, he very much doubted it.

Because what he hadn't told either Lily or Indra was that the object of his obsession, who'd disappeared from his life as abruptly as she'd entered it, was pregnant with a child which could only be his. He had tracked her whereabouts until a week ago, when she'd disappeared into thin air. But he *would* find her. He *had* to find her. Because there was no way he was allowing a child of his to be raised like he'd been—abandoned by his father and left at the mercy of hired hands.

Two months later...

PARIS CAPARELLI carefully descended the steps off the bus and adjusted her bags, which were full of grocery shopping.

"Are you all right, darlin'?" called the bus driver, a jaunty piece of tinsel in his cap, showing that at least someone was looking forward to Christmas. But not her. She appreciated the fact he didn't drive off immediately, as city drivers would have done. Although she didn't know what he'd do if she said she wasn't all right.

"I'm fine, thanks," she said, forcing a smile.

"When's your baby due?" asked the woman with neatly permed gray hair seated by the door. "Is it going to be a Christmas baby?"

"No. Due date is early January."

"Best you get home and put your feet up, my beauty," said the driver with a wave before snapping the doors closed.

Her thoughts exactly. Her back ached, and she felt sick with tiredness. She'd made the long journey to the city hospital for a check-up by public transport because her car was in the garage. Never again, she thought, rubbing her back. As usual, her gaze was drawn to the harbor which lay at the end of the narrow street, and she exhaled a calming breath. Since she'd moved into the small cottage two months earlier, she couldn't get enough of the view. The focus was the pale loop of river which formed the harbor, but beyond that, the empty marshes stretched out to the thin ribbon of sea and the vast sky. To some people, the view might seem bleak, but to her, it signified freedom. Freedom from her father and from the father of her child who, it appeared, had been tracking her every movement since she'd left the island.

Although it was only three-thirty in the afternoon, the winter sun, which had scarcely reached any height in the sky, had already descended, reduced to an outline in the misty dusk. For once, there was no wind and the pennant flags, which topped the yachts pulled up onto the muddy foreshore, were still. The reassuring, constant clacking of the flags had ceased and, as the bus disappeared with a roar around the corner, gearing up for the climb back up the hill to the main coast road, all she could hear were the lonely cries of the marsh birds.

There was no doubt about it, Blakeney Harbor in winter was a beautiful place, with an air of bleak desolation which appealed to her. She was simply thankful it didn't appeal to Harrison. He'd told her that Norfolk was the one place he hated most in the world. So what better place to hide from him?

She sighed at the thought of him. At first she'd run to avoid being trapped in the spotlight, which was Harrison's life. But then she'd kept on running when she'd discovered she was being followed. The last thing she wanted was him knowing she was expecting his baby. He'd been quite clear that he never wanted children, and there was no way she would be with anyone for the sake of a child. She'd been that child once and would never inflict what she'd endured on her own child. But while she might not want Harrison in her life, it didn't mean she could stop thinking about him. But there were more important things in her life than herself.

Her hand automatically cupped her seven-month pregnant stomach as if to protect her son. "Okay, Luca, here we go. Final assault," she murmured, picking her way carefully up the steep, cobbled lane to her terraced cottage. By the time she reached the door, the last of the light had dissolved into darkness, and her door was lit only by the streetlight from across the road.

She peered at her bunch of keys, searching for the correct one. Suddenly, she heard a car door being locked close by, followed by footsteps. She dropped the keys with a clatter on the stone step. She turned to see who it was, but there didn't appear to be anyone around. The light formed a halo around the streetlamp, hardly penetrating the chill mist which rose from the harbor. She shook herself. She was becoming scared of her own shadow. Then someone walked by and tipped his cap. A neighbor called out 'good evening' to her. Norfolk people were reputedly unfriendly, but that hadn't been her experience. But then, maybe the fact she was a young, pregnant woman, apparently alone in the world, had warmed them to her.

She reached down to pick up her keys but, by the time she'd pulled herself up, using the rusting wrought-iron railing for support, she found herself face-to-face with a man whose features she'd seen more often in her dreams than in real life.

"Harrison!" The mist swirled around him and for a moment, she thought she was imagining things. Was she dreaming, or was this a nightmare? She squeezed her eyes closed and then opened them again. But he was still there. She clutched the railing to steady herself as the blood rushed from her head and the world revolved. Then he spoke, and she realized it *was* a nightmare.

"I found you." He said it as if he couldn't believe it. For a moment the nightmare vision cleared, and she saw him, really saw him, and his eyes were exactly as they'd been when they'd made love under the Caribbean starlight—warm and caressing. But then the moment passed and his eyes hardened. "You made it hard enough," he said, a growl edging his words.

She swallowed, gripping the railing even harder. "For a reason," she said. "I didn't wish to be found."

His lip curled. "But you have been. No more running from me, Paris."

Blood pounded in her ears. She forced herself to take a deep breath. Calm. She had to be calm. "That sounds menacing," she said, unable to prevent her voice from trembling. "Now," she said, gripping her keys. "If you'll excuse me, it's getting cold and I have shopping to unpack."

She turned her back to him and, without waiting for a reply, inserted a key into the lock. It didn't work. Breathe, Paris, breathe, she said as she selected a different key and this time it clunked into place and she twisted it and opened the door.

"You can't simply walk away from me, Paris. Not again, not now."

She glanced over her shoulder at where he still stood. He hadn't moved a muscle. Hadn't tried to come closer to her. What did he hope to achieve?

"Watch me," she said, stepping inside her house, her only refuge.

Then she made a mistake and looked at him. He hadn't moved. He'd made no attempt to push past her or to hold on to her or the door. He just stood there, his eyes on her, his expression complex. And she saw the man she'd fallen for at first glance, a man she'd decided was her soul-mate at the first kiss, a man whose lovemaking had unlocked her heart. And that heart broke all over again.

He shook his head. "We need to talk."

She bit her lip and gave a quick nod, and opened the door for him to enter. The time for running was over.

CHAPTER 4

He followed her into the small sitting room, and she switched on a lamp. The warm glow, usually so comforting, now only deepened the shadows, and her uncertainty. She turned to face him.

"Why did you come?" she asked, her voice husky with fear and something else—something very much like longing.

"You know why," he said, his tall frame filling the space. "You can stand hunched up, pull your coat away from your stomach all you like, but I know you're carrying my baby."

She blanched and would have fallen as the room swam again, if he hadn't shot out a hand and steadied her. His touch felt so right. She looked up at him and they were so close she could feel his warm breath on her cheek. She opened her mouth, whether to speak or to kiss him, she couldn't have said. But he spoke first.

"You're carrying my baby," he repeated, his voice

roughened with emotion. "So I can't let you go. Besides, if I let you go now, I'm not so sure you wouldn't fall down," he added in a gentler tone.

She pushed away his hands. "I can look after myself."

"So you say. Doesn't look like it though," he said, looking around the tiny sitting room. The single lamp revealed the shabby furniture which had come with the house.

"You don't know me. We had one night together, and one night doesn't give you the right to track me down and make demands of me."

"We need to talk."

"No, we don't. We have nothing to talk about."

"You're pregnant with my child. I think that's something to talk about."

She felt her defenses cracking little by little. He was right. She *wasn't* managing well, and she was frightened about the future. And simply seeing Harrison again after so long brought back the memories which sent her fingertips tingling and her stomach flipping with desire. But being with Harrison would bring her to the world's attention—and most dangerously, her father's attention. And now the stakes were even higher.

"Paris," he said more softly. "It may only have been one night, but don't you remember that night we had together?" How could she ever forget? It had changed her life in more ways than one. "You trusted me then to come into your world, and you can trust me now. I'm not going to hurt you. I just need to talk to you. Okay?"

She nodded reluctantly. Why delay the inevitable? "Okay."

He picked up the forgotten shopping from the doorstep and placed it on the table in front of the window. He then took the few steps towards her and leaned back against the table, arms crossed. "For goodness' sake, sit down before you fall down. You look terrible."

She hadn't intended to do anything he told her, but in this case, her body agreed before she could do anything about it. And she gratefully sank into the settee, positioning a cushion in the small of her back. She wished he looked terrible, too.

"How did you find me?"

"That's irrelevant. I found you and my child. That's all I want to talk about."

"How did you find me?" she repeated, angry now, her voice steely.

He shrugged, as if the details were unimportant. "Money can buy you anything, Paris. What I don't understand is why you went to such lengths to hide from me. Was I really such an inadequate lover?"

She wished he hadn't said that, because a vision of him holding himself above her as he thrust deep inside of her filled her mind and refused to shift. She opened her mouth to speak, but licked her lips instead. Their gaze switched instantly from one of antagonism to one of connection. She shook her head and tore her gaze away.

"I had my reasons."

"Which are?"

She glared at him. "None of your business."

"You're wrong. The minute I discovered you were pregnant, you became my business, like it or not."

"I don't," she ground out.

He shrugged and pushed himself off the table. "Irrelevant." He walked around the small space, taking in the books, the bits and pieces which made up her life. "No photos." He was standing in front of her now. "No signs of a past, no signs of anyone. Just you. A woman, determined to be on her own for some reason."

"I seem to be failing at that," she said with a tight smile.

"Yes. Spectacularly."

She swallowed tightly. "So now you're here, what do you intend to do?"

"Leave this God-forsaken place and take you with me."

"I'm not coming. You've no right."

"I have every right," he said, stepping closer, his eyes blazing. "I'm our baby's father. And unless you come with me, I'll take you to court and make sure I have equal access."

She shook her head, her mouth dry with fear. It was everything she'd dreaded. "No." She swallowed hard. "No, you can't do that to me."

He inclined his head to her, and she didn't recognize him as shadows disguised his features. But then, she hardly knew him. "Oh, yes I can."

"But why would you want to? You told me you never intended to marry, nor to have children."

"Ah, so you remember. Yes, it's true. But I also hadn't intended to have unprotected sex."

She winced at his clinical words, so different to how she remembered their love-making.

"But I did," he continued. "And I have to live with the consequences. No child of mine will grow up away from me."

"That's not what *I* want."

He shrugged. "Immaterial. It's how it's going to be. I want you and our child. Get used to it, Paris. There will be no other outcome."

His words cut her to the bone.

"All *I* care about," he continued, "is that you are carrying my child and I refuse to allow that child to have the kind of upbringing which I, or any of my brothers, had. I won't allow this child to grow up without a father to protect him."

"Not even if his parents hate each other? Because that's what I grew up with, and that's exactly what I intend to avoid with my child."

He was silent for a few moments, and she could see he was struggling with something. He tightened his lips and exhaled.

"Fact is, Paris, we don't hate each other, do we? Not physically, anyway. You couldn't wait to get me into your bed seven months ago. And I'm sure it won't be long before you come begging for it again. You couldn't stay away, you were—"

"Stop it!" she shouted, and to her surprise, he did. "Please," she said, tears welling up, "stop it."

He swore under his breath, thrust his hands into his pockets and turned his back to her. She put her head in her hands and rubbed away her tears with the heels of her hands, not wanting him to see the proof of her emotions. How the hell had this happened? How had she fallen so low that her defenses against this man, who was determined to take over her life, had disintegrated? She sucked in a breath, sat up, and looked at him. As if feeling her eyes upon him, he did a half-turn and then a full turn to face her. That connection. Again. From the first moment they'd clapped eyes on each other, they'd finished each other's sentences, they'd anticipated each other's needs. It was hardly surprising, then, that he'd tracked her down. But that was where this stopped.

Unsteadily, she rose to her feet and placed a hand instinctively on her stomach, as if to protect her child from all of this. "We had a one-night stand. That's not something we can build a life on. Whatever we had, Harrison, it's in the past." His eyes narrowed dangerously, and she swallowed. "You must believe that."

"Why? When it's not true." He indicated her stomach. "A life *will* be built, whether we like it or not. And I *will* be there for my child."

He took a step towards her and she gave a small gasp, her body prickling with awareness, as if he'd trailed a finger along her bare skin, teasing and tempting her with the pleasures which simply his touch could bring. The sensation traveled deep inside of her, coming to rest in secret places where she shivered for him.

He gave a small grunt of satisfaction and lifted his hand to her face, touching her cheek with the back of his knuckles in a surprisingly tender caress. She opened her mouth as he moved towards her, readying for the kiss which would surely come. But then his eyes widened as if in shock at what he was about to do, and he paced away before realizing he had nowhere to go in that small room. He faced her, hands now firmly thrust in pockets. He looked like a man under control once more. She was glad someone was.

"It's irrelevant what we *had*, because now it's quite

clear what you *have.*" He looked at her stomach, and she cradled it possessively. "You're expecting my baby."

"Who says it's yours?" she said impulsively, desperately clinging to anything which might mean he would leave her alone. She couldn't have the kind of relationship her parents had—married because her mother had been pregnant, and regretted every day since. Everyone had suffered, including herself. She refused to let that happen to her child.

His nostrils flared, and she took a step back. She should have known how this macho man would react to such a suggestion.

"Are you saying it's someone else's?" He drew closer to her again. "Are you saying you had sex with another man?"

She wished with all her heart that she could say yes. But from the first moment she'd seen Harrison, there had been only one man for her. Trouble was, he lived a life in the public spotlight and he didn't want a family. Double strike. But she couldn't lie. She shook her head.

"No." She huffed out a deep sigh. "No, there's been no one else since you."

He relaxed visibly. "So you are saying such things to try to hurt me and send me away?"

She bit her lip and nodded.

"Okay. I get it. But you haven't hurt me." She didn't believe that. "And I'm going nowhere without you, so you'd better get used to the idea."

"You really think you're going to stay here with me?"

"No," he said, in disbelief that she could even suggest such a thing. "I've made arrangements for a more suitable property."

For a few seconds, his words conjured up a sense of security such as she'd never experienced. It was tantalizing. It was also false. She shook her head to free it of the siren's vision.

"I'm not coming with you. I'm not having a child experience a childhood like mine."

"It seems neither of us wants history to repeat itself."

She raised her eyebrows in surprised agreement. "At least that's something we can agree on."

His face softened, and he tilted his head as if trying to fathom her out. "Are you keeping well?"

She nodded. "Yes."

"When is our baby due?"

She swallowed her nerves, but there was no point in not telling him. "Two months' time."

"Right. I have a proposal to make."

Her heart skipped a beat. She'd imagined him saying those words to her in her weaker moments. But then, her fantasy had always included a man firmly out of the public eye, and the profession of undying love.

"What kind of proposal?" she asked warily.

"The kind which will give us both what we want."

"You're leaving?" she asked hopefully.

His expression soured. "No. But neither are you."

"What do you mean?"

"I mean, Paris, that we stay here, out of the public eye as you seem to want so much, but we stay together, as *I* want."

"But..." She was stunned by his suggestion of a compromise. She hadn't imagined that. "But you don't want to be tied down and you'll grow to hate me and our child will suffer because of it."

"That's a risk you'll have to take. Because there *is* no alternative. You have no other choice."

"Everyone has a choice."

"Not you. You made your choice when you kept the child."

"I could do nothing else."

He shrugged. "Whatever. The die is cast. You must come with me now."

She licked her lips as her mind raced. There were two things she feared. One was bringing her child unwelcome and unwanted into a bad relationship. But, as he said, that was a risk. The other? Harrison didn't know about that. But staying in Norfolk, out of the public eye, would avoid the other issue.

She nodded her head. "Okay. But when you say 'here', where exactly do you mean?"

"There's a house on the edge of the marshes, just outside Blakeney."

She frowned. "The large, deserted house which juts out into the marshes?"

"That's the one. It was my aunt's."

"Your aunt's?"

"Yes."

"Your aunt who played the piano."

"Yes. I only had one. She passed away over a year ago. I talked to Sebastian when I found out where you were living." He gave a mirthless smile. "It's always good to be prepared."

"But it doesn't look as if anyone has lived in it for years. It's like something straight out of a horror movie."

"Then it will be perfect for our happy little family." He

withdrew some keys from his pocket and tossed them in the air. "Get your things."

"You surely don't expect me to come now. Not this minute."

"That's exactly what I expect. Because, Paris, I'm not letting you out of my sight."

CHAPTER 5

*H*ad it really come to this, thought Paris? Being ordered around as if she were a chattel, as if she hadn't a mind of her own, as if she were a child once more, under her father's watchful eye? Harrison Richmond might be powerful and wealthy, but there was no way on this earth that he would control *her*. Her anger banished the last of her fears.

She took a step towards him, almost wondering where the fire was coming from inside of her to stand up to this man. She lifted her chin so she could look directly into his cold eyes.

"You seem to think we're living in some kind of medieval world where you can control me. You can't."

Frustration and anger glimmered in his eyes. "Paris," he growled in warning.

"What, *Harrison*?" She stressed his name. "Angry that someone is actually standing up to you for once? I am not one of your *many* girlfriends you can order around. I'm a grown woman."

"A grown woman who is carrying *my* child!" His voice thundered around the small room, but it didn't sway her. "Haven't I made myself clear? I will not have my child growing up away from me."

"Crystal clear," she said. "But it seems I haven't made *my*self clear. I have no intention of being controlled by a man ever again."

He frowned. "Who made you so afraid?"

She gasped, suddenly aware of what she'd said. "My father." She tried to move away, but he caught her hand. She'd have shaken it off if his touch had been anything but gentle. But the way he wrapped his fingers around hers, smoothing his thumb over the back of her hand, melted away the final shreds of her resistance.

"Paris? Is that why you hid away here? Not only because of me, but your father also?"

She gave one brief nod.

"You have secrets." He dropped her hand. "But they are no concern of mine. Go, get whatever you want for tonight and we'll have the rest delivered tomorrow."

"Haven't you listened to a word I've been saying? I'm not going anywhere."

"If you don't, I'll be forced to inform Signore Caparelli of your exact location."

She gasped. "You know my father's name."

"Yes, I made it my business to find out as much as I could about you. I may not know everything, but I know enough to get you to come with me, one way or another." He withdrew his phone. "You want me to do that now? Because I can."

"You'd blackmail me into coming with you?"

He shrugged. "I'll do whatever it takes. There will be no other outcome."

"You wouldn't do it."

"Try me."

She shook her head. "No, you wouldn't." But, as she watched, he held the screen of his phone out to her briefly so she could see that it showed, indeed, her father's contact details, and pressed the button. "No!" She leaped at him and finished the call before it could be answered.

"You have five minutes."

Paris felt sick as she climbed the winding staircase to her bedroom to collect what she needed. She had no choice. She'd do anything to protect her child—even if it meant going with Harrison. If she didn't, he'd tell her father, whose control over his lawless world was absolute —except over her. She'd never allow a child of hers to be connected with her father's world. Never.

IT WAS COMPLETELY dark by the time they parked at the end of a short causeway which was the only way to reach Marsh House. The house, at the very edge of the town, appeared to float above the surrounding marshes, alone and lonely. Maybe, she thought bitterly, it was the perfect place for her.

By the time she'd finished gazing up at the austere facade, and fumbling with her seatbelt, Harrison had come around to her car door and opened it. He extended his hand to her, but she slapped it away. He ignored her, gripped her hand and pulled her to standing. He released her hand immediately.

"What's the point of not accepting help when it's so obvious you need it, Paris?"

"I don't need it," she retorted quickly. "I…" she added, realizing that she did need help to get out of the low-slung car, "I just *accepted* it, then. That's all."

He collected the suitcases from the boot and led the way over the causeway. Paris shivered and glanced back at the lights of Blakeney. She felt like she was stepping into the unknown. Then an outside light came on, puncturing the darkness. She took a deep breath and approached the house. Its gray, concrete steps led up to an imposing, paneled front door, complete with a bell pull instead of a buzzer. Of course it was. She could imagine the ringing clang of the bell sounding deep inside this house, rousing servants long since dead.

"I'd offer you a hand up the steps, but I don't suppose you'll take it," Harrison said.

"I can manage the steps just fine." And she could, but only because there was a handrail.

"Be careful. I don't want you slipping, hurting the baby," he said, his face still hard, purposely trying to hurt her for her rejection of his help.

"But you don't care about hurting me, do you?" she said.

He shrugged and opened the key to the door, pushing it open wide. "Of course I do."

Hope leaped in her heart. She didn't think she had any left.

"If you get damaged, so does the baby," he added, immediately popping the fragile balloon.

Despite his angry remarks, he stood aside, his public schoolboy politeness having been ingrained in him. She stepped into the darkened hallway and to her surprise didn't smell the expected mustiness, only lavender polish and lilies.

"I thought this place had been empty for a while."

"It has."

"But all this?" She fingered the elegant petals of the lilies which stood in a Minton vase on the hall stand, then gave the highly polished oak stand a light caress. The shadowy hallway was lined with expensive rugs and revealed open doorways which disappeared into darkness. "Someone has been caring for it."

"I employed a housekeeper at the beginning of the week to come in daily and cook and clean. I have no desire to live in a deserted house."

She looked at him sharply. "You did this? You prepared all of this, believing I'd come here with you?"

"There was no *believing* about it. As I said, there was no other option. You were always coming with me."

She felt him move noiselessly up behind her. She held her breath—full of aftershave and the fresh outdoor smell of marshy salt air—as he reached behind her, brushing her arm. Her indignation faded into insignificance, drowned out by her reaction to this man in anticipation of what he might do. But, instead of a caress, he flicked on an old Bakelite switch, and the hall lit up with a brilliance its exterior didn't betray.

She released her breath with a whistle as she looked up at the elaborate crystal chandelier which hung from the center of the wood paneled hall. The exterior had suggested something dull and dingy, not an elegant, bright and luxurious interior.

"This is nothing like I imagined!" she said.

"I know. My aunt was an eccentric. She became paranoid about people knowing how wealthy she was and so the exterior remained drab—built for its surroundings, she used to say—but she kept the inside exactly as she'd inherited it from her aunt. Even changed her name." He glanced at her. "You two have more in common than I thought."

As Harrison switched on the side lights, she walked around, gazing up at the lush oil paintings of European scenes and the richly embroidered tapestry which hung against the exterior stone wall, and let her fingers trail over the priceless oversized vases.

"Aunt Beth always had those full of orchids from Richmond Manor's greenhouse. Dad continued the tradition." He looked around, lost in memories. "It always smelled of polish and flowers and her scent, Chanel No. 5."

"You sound fond of her."

"She was my aunt."

"Ah," she said facetiously, "so you're equally fond of all your relatives? You didn't sound fond of your father."

He looked away again, as if he'd been caught out. "Beth, my aunt, was…" He tailed off as if lost for words. His eyes came to rest on some photographs framed in ornate silver frames, grouped on a hall stand. "She was unique. And yes, I was fond of her."

She walked up to him and, for the first time, bridged the space between them, unable to prevent herself from touching his shoulder. He started as if she'd given him an electric shock. "You can say you're fond of someone, Harrison. Nothing bad will happen."

She'd never seen him so vulnerable. "No, you can't. If you do, they might be taken away from you."

"Is that what happened to you?"

He shrugged and stepped away, her hand falling from his shoulders. He walked over to the double doors. "Come on. I'll show you around."

It didn't look as if she were going to get anywhere by asking him personal questions. But then… that look in his eyes… Somehow she'd caught a glimpse into a side of Harrison she'd never seen. But he'd been fond of his aunt and she was only wanted for the child she carried.

Her thoughts were interrupted as she entered the main reception room. As Harrison walked around, switching on the myriad side lamps, the room slowly revealed itself. Semi-circular, with huge casement windows on three sides, the room jutted out into the marshes. Seen from the town, the unlit house had looked bleak, but inside it was anything but. Just like the hallway, it was full of treasures, and the rugs upon which she walked were thick and richly patterned. The walls, too, weren't painted, like so many modernist mansions in cool colors of gray and white, but were wallpapered in ruby red stripes, a color echoed in the thick velvet curtains which framed each of the three windows.

But her gaze stopped abruptly on the furthermost point of the room, the place where the window projected directly out onto the marshes. There, in pride of place, was a piano.

"A piano?" she exclaimed, walking up to the baby grand and brushing her hand over the handsome black teak top. She lifted the cover and ran her fingers over the keys. Something shifted inside of her and emotion welled up and blocked her throat. She swallowed, trying to rid herself of the unwanted emotion. She refused to break down in front of Harrison. She glanced up at him, only to see him quickly turn away.

"Sure," he said, with his back to her. "Music was Beth's passion."

It was hers, too. She pressed middle C and the lonely sound rang out clear and true. She lowered the cover, dropping it accidentally with a clang.

Harrison drew the thick velvet curtains against the darkness and the room transformed into a warm and elegant salon.

"You can play it, if you like."

She shook her head. "It was your aunt's—not mine." She forced a smile. "I doubt very much if she'd approve of me."

"Why?"

"I'm single, pregnant and with no means of looking after myself." She held out her hands helplessly. "I'm hardly a catch for her favorite nephew."

"She was a complicated woman." He shrugged. "Who knows whether she'd have approved."

"I guess she approved of you, if she left you this house." She couldn't prevent her lips from quirking with amusement. "And, from what I've read, you're hardly the conventional, dutiful heir-apparent."

He shot her a withering look. "I'm so flattered you've read up on me."

"Don't be. I'm curious about the man who pretended to a humble horse handler when in fact he was a notorious, polo-playing womanizer, beloved of the tabloids and known as *El hombre de corazón frío*. I'm surprised that an elderly aunt didn't disinherit you for your wild ways, or your cold heart."

"Maybe she felt sorry for me."

Her smile developed into a huffed laugh. "Sorry? For you?"

He took a step towards her and her laugh died on her lips as he gently touched her cheek. "Why not? A mother who died too young, a cruel father and a pregnant lover who deserts him? Isn't that enough to make anyone feel sorry for me? Isn't that enough to make *you* feel sorry for me?"

She knew he'd asked her a question, but her mind had ceased to work as soon as his fingers had made contact with her skin. She held her breath, wondering what he was going to do next. Not knowing whether she hoped he'd continue to touch her, whether she hoped he'd move his fingers across her skin, her lips, her neck, just as he'd done under the starlight on that faraway Caribbean island. He withdrew his hand sharply, and it was as if the light had disappeared instantly behind the ominous black cloud of his dark frown.

"Obviously not," he said, stepping away, answering his own question.

She pressed her fingers to her cheekbone where he'd touched her and then rubbed her forehead, which was beginning to throb.

"I'll take the cases upstairs. The kitchen and down-stairs bathroom are back through the hall."

She watched him leave and sank down onto one of the chintz settees, grateful it was close by. Her legs were shaking. And no wonder. What the hell was she doing there? Trapped in the splendor of this unexpected house with a man who only wanted her because she was carrying his child? A man who, it now appeared, had all the emotional range described by his nickname. Cold, indeed.

CHAPTER 6

The floorboards overhead creaked as Harrison moved around upstairs. Paris hoped he hadn't placed both suitcases in the one bedroom. Because there was no way she was going to be sleeping with him, no matter what he thought. She pressed her hand against her stomach. She could do this for her baby. For Luca. Because the alternative didn't bear thinking about. This was the lesser of two evils. If she so much as sneezed in the world outside, she risked her father finding her and forcing her to return to him. Her son would then be raised in a world of crime where love was something to be used, not cherished. She refused to bring her son into such a world.

"You look terrified," said Harrison, with a frown.

She looked up in surprise. She hadn't heard him enter the room.

"Don't flatter yourself I'm scared of you. I was merely thinking..." She trailed off as she tried to think of something with which to fob him off.

"Don't bother trying to invent a reply," he said dismissively. "I'm only interested in the truth, and you're not going to tell me that, are you?"

"I never lied to you."

"No, but you didn't tell me you were pregnant either, did you? A lie by omission is still a lie."

She shook her head. "It didn't feel like that."

"Tell me what it did feel like."

"Survival." The word fell from her lips before she'd processed the thought.

"Hm," he said, glancing away from her. "Mrs. Wright has prepared dinner for us. I suggest you eat before you do anything else. You look terrible."

Harrison might be a cold, unemotional, domineering bastard, but he was right. She felt weak and was in no doubt that she did look terrible. Although she didn't care about that. She had only one care. With one hand on her stomach, she brushed Harrison's hand away and pushed herself off the couch with her other hand.

"The dining room is this way."

She followed him back through the hall and into the second reception room, which was as grand as the sitting room. Landscape paintings of Norfolk—of marshes, glistening in the clear Norfolk light, and the cool, mint-green, ever-changing sea—lined its walls. The large table, on which three silver candelabra took pride of place, dominated the room.

"Looks like she loved Norfolk," said Paris, easing herself into the nearest seat. "It's an homage to the marshes."

"She did. Although she wasn't raised here."

Paris was curious about the woman whose influence

she sensed in the interior decor, and who loved Chopin as she did.

"Where did she grow up?"

"On the family estate with my mother."

"So, how did she end up here? On the edge of the world?" she murmured, aware of the nothingness which lay between her and the sea, a mile across the marshes.

"She moved here when she was in her twenties, after her aunt left the place to her. She never got on with my father—not surprising, no one did—and so I'd come here to see her."

"And your father allowed it?"

"My father couldn't have cared less what we boys did after Mother died. He only allowed us home from boarding school twice a year for summer and Christmas holidays. All other holidays, we had to stay at school." He shook his head. "My brothers were happy to, because they escaped his anger and punishments. I was the youngest and so missed most of his abuse. And, when my aunt invited us to come here, Sebastian and Alexander usually refused. They were too busy seducing local girls and getting drunk in the village pubs. But I'd come," he added quietly.

"But I thought you hated Norfolk. You told me you did."

He glanced at her and opened the old-fashioned warming drawer, releasing a mouth-watering aroma.

"And so I suppose that's why you came here?" he said.

She nodded.

"Coincidence that you made Blakeney your home."

"I drove around Norfolk, trying to figure out where to settle, and fell in love with Blakeney at first sight."

He was silent for a few moments. "Maybe not a coincidence, then." Before she could ask him what he meant, he continued quickly. "I avoided Richmond Manor because of the bad memories and here, Marsh House, because of the good ones." He pressed his lips together as if trying to stop something from emerging. Paris knew what that felt like. It seems they'd both been taught from an early age that the only good emotion was a repressed one. And that had always been fine by her. Emotion got you nowhere. Only opened you up, made you vulnerable to rejection. He cleared his throat. "But no, I've never hated this place," he continued. "In fact, it's the one place that feels like home."

"And yet you avoided it."

"It's easier that way."

"The easy way isn't always the best way."

He poured himself a glass of wine and took a drink.

"You should eat," he said, sitting back in his chair. "You're wasting away."

She tapped her stomach. "Hardly."

"You know what I mean. Your face is thinner and your arms…" He seemed to have to wrest his gaze from them.

She could point out that her breasts were twice their normal size, but she hardly wanted to bring his attention to her breasts right at that moment. Or ever. Instead, she ate. And once she'd taken a bite, she mentally thanked the housekeeper and kept on eating. She'd been rationing her shopping until now, because her removal expenses had eaten into her frugal budget. At least housekeeping was one thing less to worry about.

Harrison only picked at his food and eventually settled

back in his chair, cradling his wine and watching her. It was unsettling, but she refused to react.

Once she'd finished eating, she rose and picked her plate up to take it into the kitchen.

He reached out his hand. "Leave that. The housekeeper will deal with it."

"Is that all you expect me to do? Eat and sleep while my baby grows inside of me?"

"Yes."

"I've news for you. I've also got a life to live, whether you like it or not. Which means I won't be sitting around here all day like a beached whale."

"You will have other things to do."

"Like what? Hey?" She put her hands on her hips. "Listen to your every word, fawn over you? Is that how you imagine life will be?"

He shrugged. "No. But if that's what you'd like to do, it's fine by me. No, I was referring to the contractor I've hired. You'll need to liaise with her over the arrangements."

"Contractor? What contractor? What arrangements?"

"The wedding planner." She gasped. He rose slowly and stood over her. "You surely didn't expect me to allow you to have our child outside of marriage?"

She shook her head. "You know what? I did. I hardly took you to be a stickler for convention. A convention which, it seems to me, involves practically kidnapping me and holding me here before we get married. Have I missed anything out?"

"No," he said, his lip twitching with a rare smile. "I think that sums it up."

She grunted in frustration. "You're impossible."

"It's been said."

She pushed her chair under the table. "I'm going to bed. If you'll allow me to, of course. Perhaps you'd like me to ask permission?"

"Sure. You can go to bed."

She clenched her fists by her side. "I was *not* asking permission!" She swore under her breath and he frowned. She swore again, turning on her heel, and stormed out of the room.

She leaned heavily on the wooden staircase as she ascended the stairs. Once on the landing, she looked around, not knowing which was her room. She opened the first door she came to and peered inside. A large medieval-style four-poster bed dominated the otherwise austere room. She walked to the window, drawn by the lights of Blakeney, which twinkled on the far side of the causeway. The tide had risen, and she suddenly saw what she'd feared. That she was trapped on an island with Harrison.

"This isn't your room," Harrison said from the doorway.

"No, I guessed not. No bags, for one thing."

"And for another?"

"It looks like a man's room. Masculine."

"It was my aunt's husband."

"I didn't realize she married."

"Briefly. He died in an accident." He stepped into the room and went to another door, which Paris hadn't seen before. "Here's your room." He opened a door which led directly into another bedroom.

She walked over to him. "How handy for you. Half-a-dozen steps and you'll be in my bed."

She regretted her words even before the last syllable had dropped. The atmosphere changed instantly. She could see it in his eyes, in the way he opened his mouth as if about to say her name, in the way his hand flexed as if he had difficulty in stopping himself from reaching out to her. Would he take her in his arms, like he'd done that night under the palm trees with only the stars to witness their embrace? Would he hold her, take away her night-mares, and keep her safe? But wasn't that what he believed he was doing? Keeping her safe? The moment passed, and he stepped away.

"Sleep well," he said, opening the door for her. She stepped inside. The side lights of the beautiful, wood paneled room were already lit, but the curtains were open to the dark of the night. A light rain pattered again the window pane. Outside, she knew, were the wild marshes which had first drawn her to the place. She suddenly remembered.

"Harrison, what did you mean when you said that maybe it wasn't a coincidence that I chose Blakeney?"

"My aunt told me once that she fell in love with Blakeney at first sight. Seems you two have more in common than just pianos and me."

He closed the door behind him and she was left alone with the thought—both comforting and challenging—that it was no coincidence she was here. No, it was something much more like fate. It seemed she was fated to be as lonely as Aunt Beth. She might not be alone, but she knew from first-hand experience that a marriage and children didn't prevent loneliness. It often caused it.

And, as she heard his footsteps descend the stairs, she thought she was more alone now than she'd ever been before.

The next morning Paris awoke with a start and sat up, wondering where on earth she was. A strip of bright light had forced its way through a gap in the thick curtains, cutting across the dark floorboards and the muted tones of the old silk rug, before coming to rest on the cream quilt.

Marsh House. Harrison.

The memories of the previous day tumbled in on her, and she lay back on the soft pillows. She was surprised to discover she didn't feel as unsettled as she thought she'd be. She guessed a good night's sleep could do that for you.

The bed was enormous and, like Harrison's next door, was a four-poster, except this one was definitely more feminine. Its sturdy wooden posts were draped with the lightest of cream voile, patterned with fleur de lis. The same pattern was printed on the finest Egyptian cotton sheets, which smelled of lavender. Harrison's Aunt Beth obviously had great taste and her home had been well cared for. You could know someone by the things with which they surrounded themselves, mused Paris. Like Beth. Her taste was eclectic—with decorations, trinkets, and furniture collected from all over the world—but her love of flowers and fine aesthetic sense united them. There was nothing brash or jarring in the house. You could also know a person by whom they loved most in the world. Because Paris was in no doubt that Harrison had been the apple of his aunt's eye and that she'd done her level best to give him the love of which he'd been deprived. Goodness knows what he'd been like if he hadn't received it.

She sighed at the thought of the conundrum that was Harrison. She'd fallen for a man who didn't exist. When she'd first met him, she'd immediately felt a deep connection with him. But it had been based on a lie. He lived the kind of life—public, shallow and heartless—that was the opposite of what she wanted. And, to prove the point, he'd given her no other option but to move in with him. Again, the opposite of what she wanted. Was she never going to be rid of men wanting to control her?

With a sigh, she rose from the bed, unhooked her robe from the back of the door and pulled it around herself the best she could. She padded over to the window, swept aside the curtains and looked out to a world on fire. She huffed a laugh at the ridiculous beauty of the sun's rich rays which spilled over the marshes, setting them aflame. As if to celebrate the morning, a flock of geese swooped by. She flung up the sash window and shivered at the cold, but was spellbound by the sound of a shore lark and the boom of a bittern. Suddenly, their calls were joined by another, far more familiar sound. She glanced around to see her phone vibrating gently on the bedside table.

It was a message from Harrison. Apparently, breakfast would be in one hour. One hour *precisely*, she imagined. She grunted dismissively, tossed the phone onto the bed and returned to the window, willing the peace she saw outside to enter her again. Instead, she saw someone walking along the raised path from the sea toward the house. And not just any someone. Harrison was wearing an old tweed jacket and had his head down, as if lost in thought. His dark, curly hair flicked in the breeze. He looked impossibly handsome. Like a model on a fashion shoot, albeit it a grumpy one. He looked up suddenly, and she was subjected to the full force of those vivid blue eyes.

Paris spun away from the window, embarrassed at being caught watching him and stunned by how his direct gaze could cause her heart to pound so rapidly. How did one simple glance have the power of his physical touch? Impossible! Except it wasn't.

Her rapid heartbeat reminded her of when she'd been a girl, growing up in her restrictive Italian father's household, subjected to the violent clashes between her parents. Then it had been fear which had ignited it, which had made her run and keep on running. Now? It wasn't fear, it was something much more dangerous. Something which could trap her more firmly than anything which had come before. She was like a fly caught by a spider, trapped by its sticky threads. Every time she moved, the threads seemed to tighten around her, ensnaring her even further. But she had no choice, she reminded herself. It wasn't for her. It was for her baby.

With that reminder firmly embedded in her brain, Paris entered the adjoining bathroom and switched on the shower. She had an appointment to keep. He might have got her here under duress, but if he thought he was going to create a timetable for her, he had another think coming.

SHOWERED, dressed and hungry, Paris introduced herself to Marie, the person responsible for the well-kept house. She turned out to be a thirty-something woman who was already hard at work baking, preparing dinner and cleaning, apparently all at the same time. Paris was grateful. She felt too tired to do anything. She'd heard a lot about how pregnant women should do yoga, swim and keep fit. But all she wanted to do now was lie down and eat. She guessed she wasn't a poster-girl for pregnancy. She also guessed she was probably more typical. She picked up a tea towel and began drying some crockery to show willing.

Their conversation was interrupted by the sound of a heavy tread walking along the hall before entering the dining room.

Marie smiled cheerfully. "Don't worry about that lot," she said. "You join Mr. Richmond and I'll bring along full English breakfasts. Coffee is on the table and I'll bring in some freshly brewed tea."

"I don't want to put you to any extra bother."

Marie smiled. "It's no bother at all. That's what I'm paid for—to look after you both, so you mustn't stop me from doing my job."

Paris shot her an answering smile, relieved. She'd found an ally in Marie and felt a little less alone. "I won't. And thank you."

Paris was struck once more by the grandeur of the dining room, with its wood paneling and landscape paintings hanging from the picture rail. Harrison was pouring himself a coffee from the side table.

"Would you like a cup?" he asked, glancing at her.

"No thanks. Marie is bringing in some tea." She glanced at the table settings at either end of the large table. It reminded her of the formality of her father's house. She turned to the view from the window instead. This room looked out toward the small town which climbed up the steep hill away from the harbor. It seemed incredible to Paris that people were going about their everyday life while her life had changed so dramatically overnight. There were women dragging shopping trolleys up the hill to the butchers, children tugging at each other and laughing as they ran to catch the school bus, and some boats already being launched on the high tide from the quayside. She'd always yearned for the ordinary, but had never been able to find it.

"You slept well," he said. It was a statement.

"It seems your knowledge knows no bounds," she said. "Tell me, what did I dream of?"

He shot her a dark look. "It doesn't take a mind-reader to see that you're better rested. I know your face well."

"Really? I'm surprised."

"You're surprised?"

He took a few steps closer. It wasn't an aggressive movement, more as if he were simply drawn to her. She knew because she felt the same compulsion, but she refused to bridge the gap between them.

She nodded. "We were together for such a short time. And yet you know my face? Unlikely, I'd have thought."

He looked away from her for the first time, out the window, but he wasn't looking at the view. She could tell his thoughts were far away. She exhaled in relief. Being under his gaze was like being in a spotlight.

"That morning in Hermosa, dawn must have come around five. You'd fallen asleep on my arm, your hair over my chest. I don't know how many hours passed before you awoke, but believe me, I studied your face and I know it."

Her mouth suddenly dried as her memory took her back to their time together. He looked back at her with a different expression on his face. Softer.

"And this morning you look more like you did then. Rested. Though still too thin," he said.

His implied criticism broke the spell

"The light wasn't good in the beach house. I really don't think you know me as well as you think you do. We spent most of our time in the dark."

He placed his coffee cup on the table and walked up to her, studying her features for a moment before reaching out and lightly brushing his fingers against her cheek. Everything stopped—her thoughts, her breathing, every-thing—except the sensation his fingers created as he caressed her skin.

"In the dark? It was then that I knew you best of all, because I could feel you beneath my fingers, beneath my body. Skin to skin. You can't deny it, Paris, I know you. Whether you want me to or not."

She opened her mouth to speak but closed her eyes instead as he brushed his thumb briefly over her cheek, and then his touch left her. The door opened, and Marie came in with a trolley of food and a big smile.

Paris hastened to the dining table and engaged Marie in conversation. She felt humiliated that simply his touch could transform her into a quivering mess.

"Well, I hope you enjoy your breakfast," said Marie. "And if there's nothing else, I'll be off now."

She felt his arm around her shoulders. "Thank you, Marie," he said.

He pulled out a chair for her. What she'd first thought of as charming old-school politeness, she now interpreted as part of his controlling nature.

"Harrison," she said decisively, as soon as she could hear Marie moving around in the kitchen. "I'd like you to stop that."

He took the seat at the opposite end of the table and glanced at her in surprise. "Stop what?"

She waved her hand. "This flirtation, or whatever you want to call it. That wasn't part of the deal. I've agreed that you can share in our child's upbringing. I haven't agreed to anything else."

To her irritation, he smiled. Or, rather, his lips didn't move, but a flare of amusement lit his eyes.

She folded her arms onto the table. "And what do you find so amusing about that?"

"You may not approve of my methods, Paris. You may not even like me very much, but you have to admit we have a physical connection like no other."

The blush began in the pit of her stomach and swept up over her chest, not stopping until it suffused her cheeks with its telltale answer. She could hardly refute what her body had so obviously agreed to.

"That's irrelevant." Her voice sounded strained. Calm, she told herself. Keep calm. "Irrelevant," she emphasized. "This is a business-like arrangement and it will remain business-like."

He shrugged. "We'll see."

She tossed down her serviette in frustration. "There you go again! No, we *won't* see. There won't be any..." She trailed off, unwilling to express the traitorous visions which had slammed into her head.

He raised an eyebrow. "Any?"

"That's right. There won't be any of that."

"Right. Purely business-like then."

"Exactly. So, don't think you have to keep me company at breakfast, or at any other time. Your polo career presumably doesn't run itself. I'm sure you have work to do."

He shook his head. "No," he replied, helping himself to butter and pouring another coffee. He offered one to her. She shook her head, frustrated. "I've retired from polo."

"Why?" she asked, fighting a rising panic.

He took a bite of toast and chewed it while contemplating her. Eventually, he swallowed. The tension increased with every passing second.

"For God's sake, why?"

"Because, Paris, I intend to have a very different family life from that of my father."

"Why? What kind did he have?" She hardly dared ask, but she had to know.

His face hardened. "A distant one." He folded his arms, leaned on the table, and fixed her with his gaze. "And I have no intention of being distant. I will be close by—you and our child—every step of the way." He wiped his mouth on the serviette and rose and went out of the room.

A shiver tracked her spine. It was exactly what she'd feared, and what she'd spent her whole life running from.

*P*aris sat at the breakfast table for a few moments longer, head in hands, trying to breathe through the impending panic attack. She could hear him moving around the kitchen and then enter the library. She needed to talk to him whether she wanted to or not. She needed to create some space for herself.

Harrison was standing, resting his hands on the desk, leaning over the computer in the library.

"Harrison," she said quietly.

He twisted to look at her. "I'm not going anywhere, Paris, and you may as well get used to the idea."

"But what about your work? Your horses?"

"I've pulled out of all competitions."

"You've what?"

"Pulled out of the circuit. For this year anyway."

"But why?"

"I'd have thought that was obvious."

"Not to me, it's not."

"Because, Paris, we are having a baby."

"A baby doesn't mean that parents have to stop work."

"Some might. Lucky for me, my career was more of a pastime and I've enough money to do what I like."

She could hardly contradict him there. Her online research had revealed exactly how wealthy he was. Another similarity to her father and another strike against him.

"Although," he continued, "you're not making our new life easy to negotiate. What with all the secrecy, which is beyond me. But I'll humor you for now and we'll keep a low profile as you wish. For now. But once the baby is born, we'll move on."

"What if I don't want to move on?" The thought of moving back into the world where her father could track her down filled her with panic. "I mean," she quickly said, not wanting Harrison to question her, "your aunt lived here all her life."

"Not all her life. She lived in Paris for a while."

"Paris! That must be where she got her clothes from. I noticed them in the wardrobe. They're all couture and exquisite. I'm surprised they're still there."

He shrugged. "I gave instructions for everything to stay the same."

"Including the piano," she noted.

She put down his lack of response to his sudden interest in an incoming email.

While he was distracted, she took the opportunity to look around the library. Apparently, his aunt had preferred a traditional, masculine-looking library. There were no feminine touches to relieve the rows of dark red, brown, and black leather-bound books. The colors were echoed in the leather chairs and velvet drapes. It was a scene straight out of a Victorian television drama. She glanced at Harrison who was staring at his computer. She knew he wanted her to leave, but she was curious about his aunt.

"So, what brought your aunt back here, to Norfolk?"

He sighed and looked up from the computer. "A love affair gone wrong. Or something like that. I can't say I ever asked, and she wasn't forthcoming. But I vaguely recall Sebastian saying something of the sort."

"Oh, that's so sad."

He steepled his fingers and looked at her. "Is it? Then why do you wish to repeat history? *A love affair gone wrong.* Why do you want to remain a recluse, hidden away on the edge of the marshes with nothing between you and the North Pole? A tad dramatic, don't you think? It's fine for a few months, but there's a big world out there."

She looked away, gritting her teeth stubbornly. "I don't look at it like that."

"Maybe Beth didn't, either."

She'd strayed into dangerous territory. Time she left.

"Well, as lovely as it's been chatting with you, I must get on. I have things to do, even if you haven't."

"Ah, you mean your hospital appointment?" he said.

"How do you know about that?"

"I contacted the hospital to arrange an appointment for you and they informed me you already have one."

"That's my business."

"Wrong." He rose and tossed his serviette onto the table. "That's *our* business. We need to leave in half an hour."

"I know that," she said angrily. "I have a taxi coming

and I will take it to Norwich and have my scan as planned."

He sighed and shook his head, as if he were dealing with a stubborn child.

"What? Don't tell me you've canceled the taxi too?" she said.

"I'm glad you're getting the picture."

"I am. And the picture is framed, solidly, so that nothing can escape." She took a step closer to him, her anger and indignation and fear giving her the nerve. "You've got to back off. I can hardly breathe. You're suffocating me."

"I'm caring for our child."

"Wrong," she said, walking away angrily. "You're caring for yourself. Don't mistake the two."

She slammed the door and hurried upstairs. Grabbing her make-up bag, she furiously applied some mascara, swearing as she smudged it. She wiped it away with a tissue and stared at her flushed face in the mirror. She had to calm down, because she had no choice *but* to travel to her appointment with Harrison. She could do this. She *had* to do this for her child.

Harrison was waiting by the car on the other side of the causeway, looking across the creek toward the village as if he didn't have a care in the world. But then he didn't, she thought to herself as she walked to the car. It was she who shouldered the cares.

They drove the half-hour journey in silence. Somehow he found a park directly outside the hospital—of course he did, she thought huffily—and they entered the building together. He, with his arm around her, opening doors and guiding her, as if she'd break.

The silence continued inside. It was on the tip of her tongue to ask him to wait outside, but she didn't want to cause a scene and she knew Harrison would have yet another answer ready for her. She couldn't fight him on this. He looked as implacable and as unemotional as always, which, she reckoned, made it easier for him to always be one step ahead.

Inside the consulting room, the silence was eased by the soothing talk of the sonographer, who was obviously accustomed to handling sensitive situations. She shifted her gaze from Harrison, whose air of complete dominance continued to infuriate her, to the sonographer, who talked reassuringly about what they were about to see. She jumped as he smeared cool gel onto her stomach and then all eyes were on the screen, which flickered into life. She'd already had one scan and everything had been fine, so hadn't expected to learn anything new from this one. Which had been a mistake, because she wasn't prepared for how big the baby would be. *Her* baby. Luca. She sat forward, intent on learning every curve and line of her baby boy as he appeared on the screen, only half-listening to the sonographer's murmurings.

The clatter of a chair falling onto the floor made her turn suddenly. Harrison stood, mouth slightly open, staring at the screen as if he were looking at a television for the first time, his expression a blend of shock and incomprehension. He pointed to an angular shape on the monitor. "What the hell is that? Is it a..." He trailed off and looked at the sonographer, whose lips tweaked with amusement but otherwise kept a professional manner. "It's an elbow, Mr. Richmond."

"Oh. But it *is* a boy, though."

"Yes, it's a boy."

"Luca," said Paris with a smile, as if greeting her son for the first time. She ignored the indignant grunt from Harrison. They hadn't had a chance to talk about anything much, let alone names. But Luca's name wasn't up for discussion. "He looks bigger than I imagined."

"He's developing nicely," said the sonographer. "But he does look as if he'll be a good weight. Have you made plans for your birth?"

"I want a natural birth," she said. "But in hospital." She'd have preferred it to be at home but, given the fact she currently lived on the edge of a marsh, miles from the nearest hospital and knew no one other than Harrison, she didn't think it would be practicable. And she doubted Harrison had ever helped deliver a baby before.

"Of course it will be in the hospital," said Harrison. She gritted her teeth. Harrison's eyes were firmly on the screen. He shook his head. "It's amazing. I hadn't imagined…" He broke off and looked away from the screen and Paris, before hurrying out the room.

The sonographer smiled conspiratorially at her. She wasn't sure why. She was annoyed that Harrison upped and left, as if he had no desire to see anything further. As she continued to ask questions about the baby, the sonographer printed off some images from the scan and handed them to her.

She smiled to herself as she traced the line of Luca's cheek and his shoulder, his eyes. She couldn't wait to hold him. It wouldn't be long now. She sniffled and a bunch of tissues were thrust in front of her. She looked up. She hadn't heard Harrison return to the room.

He checked his watch and stepped away, with barely a glance at her.

"You'd better wipe away those tears and get dressed. We're running late."

Her mouth fell open, but there were no words to describe how she felt. He was so unemotional and cold, the chill invaded her. If he was like this now, when they were doing something which should have brought them closer, what the hell would he be like as the months rolled into years? But she knew the answer. As she watched him leave the room, she stood up and pulled on her jersey. She knew what they'd both be like. They'd be her worst nightmare. Two parents who hated each other and resented each other, and a child caught in the middle.

But what the hell was she going to do about it? As she re-did her ponytail, pulling back the hair sharply, she recognized the fierce look in her eyes. It was the expression of someone fighting for her child.

CHAPTER 9

$\mathcal{P}$aris stormed out of the hospital, ahead of Harrison. Once in the car, she turned to him.

"We need to talk."

He glanced at her in surprise. "What about?"

"Isn't it obvious?"

"Not to me, it's not," he said, starting up the engine and pulling out of the carpark.

"I want to talk about *us*. I want to talk about *Luca*."

"Yes, what's this all about Luca for a name? We hadn't agreed on one."

"There is no discussion about his name. It's Luca, and that's that. I've always loved the name, and it's a nod to my Italian heritage."

"I'd prefer something more British."

"And *I* wouldn't. There will be no discussion."

He humphed. "I thought you wanted to talk."

"Not about my son's name."

"*Our* son's name."

"And *that* is what I want to talk about. That we can't

talk without sniping at each other. I won't have a marriage like my parents!"

"Why not? What was wrong with it?"

"They hated each other."

"Then why did they get together?"

"Because my mother wanted to marry my father because he was wealthy, and made sure she became pregnant."

"History repeating itself," he murmured as he flicked the indicator and drove out onto the main road.

Was it possible to become angrier? She didn't think so. "I did *not* get pregnant on purpose."

He gave an ambiguous grunt.

"What does that grunt mean?"

"It's a grunt. It doesn't mean anything."

"Sounded like it meant something to me."

He sighed. "Like what?"

"Like you don't believe me."

"Of course I believe you. I simply meant a marriage brought about by a pregnancy. I hardly think you'd have covered your tracks so well if you wanted to marry me."

The wind left her sails, and she sat back in her chair. "No, believe it or not, I didn't want a child at all. Until I discovered I was pregnant." She caressed her stomach. "And then there was suddenly no question what to do."

"Run away and hide," he said coldly.

She fixed her gaze straight ahead. "But you stopped that, didn't you?"

"Yep," he said, turning off the highway, and onto one of the minor roads which criss-crossed the countryside.

She frowned, checking the signposts.

"This isn't the way to Blakeney."

"Correct."

"Where are we going?"

"To Richmond Manor. My sister-in-law is keen to meet you."

"Your sister-in-law? Harrison, when did you tell them about me?" She felt queasy at the thought that Harrison had been spreading the news that he'd found her, far and wide. If he had, it would only be a matter of time before her father found her. It was no good, she'd have to tell Harrison. And soon.

"Sebastian rang this morning. Seems his lovely wife, Indra, was curious why I was staying at Marsh House. I don't know why you're so riled. They're going to know soon enough. I can hardly marry you *and* keep you quiet."

Marry. The word hit her like the final nail in a coffin. She opened her mouth to speak, but no words emerged. She shook her head and stared, unseeing, at the passing countryside. It *would* happen. Harrison would make sure of it. And a part of her—a tiny part that had sprung into life early in their relationship and had refused to die— welcomed it. That she'd wanted him wasn't in dispute. What she *didn't* want—what her worst nightmare conjured up—was a marriage of bickering transforming into a relationship based on hatred with their child at best a pawn, at worst a scapegoat. But her worst nightmares were coming true. And, if her in-laws were anything like Harrison, they were about to get worse.

HARRISON WONDERED for the nth time why he felt the need to introduce Paris to Sebastian and Indra. It was reasonable, of course. He was marrying Paris, they were having a baby, and she would be part of the family. *Family*. The very word made him huff derisively. He'd had little to do with his brothers growing up. They'd each attended different public schools and had had even less to do with his father. He could hardly remember a time when his mother had been alive. His brothers could, and he'd always felt jealous of their memories. He had nothing. Only a distant, cold father and institutions which soon made him stop showing any sign of emotion, because there was no point. There had been no one to come to him when he'd cried himself to sleep in his dorm, and there had been no one to confide in when his father had told him he wasn't welcome at home in the holidays. His Aunt Beth had been the only person who'd shown him any attention and he could hardly say that had been over-emotional. His family simply didn't go in for emotion and that was that. If that was what Paris wanted, then she'd be disappointed.

They drove the rest of the way in silence, through the narrow, hedgerow-lined lanes, deeper into rural Norfolk. Paris had obviously decided silence was better than arguing, and he had to agree. But, when they turned the corner and drove along the lane which skirted the Richmond Estate and the trees parted to reveal the house, Paris leaned forward, and gave a low whistle.

"What a beautiful house."

"Richmond Manor," he said, as they drove up the tree-lined avenue.

She glanced at him in surprise before leaning forward again, peering up at the manor at the end of the avenue. Its Georgian proportions looked their best, framed by the dark tangle of trees on either side—their branches stark and clearly outlined against the bright blue sky.

"Your family home is seriously cool."

A part of him relaxed. He hadn't even realized he was tense. But without the undercurrent of anger and disagreement which usually accompanied her words, she sounded like the Paris he'd first met, the Paris he couldn't be without.

He shrugged, not prepared to show her how happy it made him she'd reacted this way. "It's not my home."

"No, but it was yours growing up, wasn't it?"

"Nominally. I spent most of my time at school, or at Marsh House."

He sensed her eyes on him and knew they'd be full of curiosity, but he refused to meet her gaze, or answer the unasked questions.

"Hm," she said, glancing away.

"What do you mean, hm?" he said, unable to erase the irritation from his voice.

"Just thinking that it figures."

He ground his teeth, knowing exactly what she meant.

He was institutionalized and unfeeling. So what if he was? She'd have to get used to it.

He swung the car in front of the house and pulled on the handbrake too firmly. "I'm so glad you have every-thing figured out."

She shot him a dark look. "Not everything. Not yet. But I will."

He didn't know what she meant exactly, and he really didn't want to know. All he wanted was for Paris to accept the situation they found themselves in, without kicking and screaming every step of the way.

"Perhaps we could suspend hostilities until after our visit to my brother and his family?"

She bit her lip but gave a quick nod of agreement.

The front door burst open and the sound of a wailing baby emerged, quickly followed by Sebastian holding the crying baby in his arms. He didn't seem in the least perturbed by the screaming as he came down the steps towards them, a beaming smile on his face. Harrison didn't think he'd ever seen his brother look so happy.

"Harrison!" Sebastian called out. Harrison stepped out of the car and stuck out his hand to shake his brother's, but was instead offered a crying baby. It seemed he had no choice but to accept as Sebastian moved around the car to greet Paris.

"Hey!" called Harrison, holding up the baby, who took one look at him and sucked in more air with which to scream. "Don't leave me with this!"

"This?" said Sebastian, stepping towards Paris, as she slammed the car door closed. "*This* is my darling daughter, Charlotte." Ignoring Harrison, Sebastian turned his charm on Paris. "When Harrison said he was bringing his fiancée to Richmond, I thought he was joking. But here you are." His eyes dropped to her stomach as her coat flew open in the wind. "Here you *both* are," he amended with a smile. Harrison suspected his brother didn't mean him and Paris, but Paris and the child. He hadn't told Sebastian that Paris was pregnant. What was the point? It would be crystal clear when they met.

Harrison watched as Sebastian greeted Paris and Paris instantly shed her reserve, unfurling like a flower in the sun. He was pleased to see her relax and regain some of her old self, but also annoyed that she wasn't like that with him. But his attention was quickly diverted to the screaming child, who he struggled to pacify. He tried to remember what people did with babies and gave it a little jiggle. The screaming lessened and, encouraged, he jiggled it some more. Finally, the screaming reduced to a hiccup and her eyelids closed.

"Harrison!" called Indra, emerging from the path which led from the estate offices and the stables. "How lovely to see you!" She came up to him and first kissed her daughter on the forehead, softly so she wouldn't awaken, and then Harrison on both cheeks. "Thank you so much for coming! I wasn't sure you'd be able to make it."

"Yes, well, it's been a little complicated."

Indra glanced over to where Sebastian and Paris were walking towards the house, not having noticed Indra's arrival.

"I can see that. You kept your young lady pretty quiet."

"I had good reason."

"Want to share?"

He thought for a moment. "The only thing I want to share is your child, Indra."

He handed her back to Indra, who immediately forgot about the conversation which he didn't want to have.

"And this is my wife, Indra," said Sebastian to Paris.

"Pleased to meet you," said Paris with a smile, which was warmly returned by Indra.

"And you. This is a lovely surprise. Come on inside, Paris. I bet your back is aching. I know mine was when I was pregnant."

Harrison watched Indra and Paris disappear inside and then looked up at the manor house, which represented everything about family he didn't want. Even with his eldest brother and wife happily ensconced there now, it was hard to change the deep-rooted feelings he had about the place.

A hefty clap on the back from Sebastian interrupted his thoughts.

"You handed the apple of my eye back to Indra pretty damned quick. I'd have thought you could use the practice."

"There will be plenty of time for that later. Besides, we'll have staff to take care of it."

Sebastian shook his head and grinned. "I can't wait to watch you do one big U-turn on that!" He laughed. "Staff indeed. He or she will be your kid, your child, and you'll want to take care of it, not hand it over to someone. Well, not all the time, anyway."

Harrison raised an unamused eyebrow. "Whatever."

Sebastian frowned and stopped mid-step. "It *is* your child, isn't it?"

"Of course it's my child. I'd hardly be doing all of this if it weren't."

"There's no *of course* about it. If there's one thing I've discovered over the past few years, it's that, just when you think you've got life sorted, it throws you a series of curve balls and all you can expect is the unexpected."

"You're right about that."

"Anyway, it's good to see you again. I couldn't figure out why you wanted to stay at Marsh House. I thought you weren't telling us everything."

Harrison shrugged. He wasn't used to sharing his thoughts with anybody, let alone a member of his family. He guessed times were changing. "I wasn't hiding anything. Just forgot to mention it."

"Well, I'm pleased. It's about time you stopped wandering the world, screwing women left, right and center, and found someone to love."

"I think you've taken a leap too far."

Sebastian's lips quirked into a smile. "Whatever. I'll leave you to sort that out. Anyway," he said, opening the front door and stepping inside, "it's good to have you back again. I'm seeing more of you and Alexander than I have in years. Happy families, eh?"

Harrison couldn't answer that in the affirmative, so stayed silent. They continued through the hall and into the drawing room, where he could hear Indra and Paris talking.

Sebastian immediately went to Indra as if drawn like a magnet. Harrison paused in the doorway, looking at the three of them, chatting as naturally as if they were long-lost friends.

As if aware he was watching her, Paris looked around while Indra and Sebastian cooed over the baby. Their gazes met. He glanced away too quickly. He could see she was curious, but about what exactly, he wasn't sure. No doubt he'd find out eventually.

Tea and cake were served and as time passed, Harrison could see a bond forming between Paris and Indra and Sebastian which surprised him. He'd accepted his brother's invitation, assuming it was nothing more than both a polite gesture and a way to satisfy Indra's curiosity. He hadn't imagined this, and wasn't sure how he felt about it.

With baby Charlotte now sleeping peacefully in the crib, a comfortable silence had settled over them. Harrison was content to watch Paris flicking through an old photograph album, which Sebastian had insisted he show her, presumably in an attempt to embarrass Harrison. It seemed sibling rivalry never died. He didn't mind. He liked how well she was getting on with them both.

"So, you want to get married here?" Indra asked.

Harrison glanced at Paris, who bit her lip and looked away. He cleared his throat. "Yes. Obviously, for the baby, we're going to marry." Paris cleared her throat and Indra gave a light tut, as if she disapproved of his sentiment. "And," he continued, ignoring their reactions, "if it's okay with you, I thought here would be most suitable, more private."

Sebastian sat forward, hands clasped before him. "That will be great. I've mentioned it to the vicar who will take the service. He'll be in touch with you over the arrangements."

"Good." Harrison chanced a look at Paris, who closed the photo album without finishing it. He looked back at Sebastian, deciding to ignore Indra whose eyes he could feel boring accusingly into him. "It seemed best," he added, not sure what to say next to dig himself out of the hole he apparently found himself in.

"Best for whom?" asked Indra.

He sighed and looked at her. Her eyes were blazing.

"For us both," he said with deliberate patience.

Indra turned to Paris and her expression warmed. She impulsively reached out and took Paris's hand and gave it a squeeze. "You're not to worry about anything. I'm happy to organize everything for you," said Indra.

"There's nothing for Paris to worry about. I've hired someone," said Harrison.

"Then un-hire them," shot back Indra. "It's no problem for me to organize it. It'll be easy because I'm on the spot."

It was Harrison's turn to feel indignant. "Everything is under control."

"Including Paris," said Indra without thinking. She exchanged a meaningful glance with Sebastian. "I'm sorry," she added. "All I mean is that I assume you're like Sebastian and under the misapprehension that you can control everything around you—including us women." She smiled at Paris, who returned her smile, obviously relieved to have found a kindred spirit.

Harrison didn't know Indra well, although she was his step-sister as well as sister-in-law. Life could be complicated sometimes. And he was beginning to *not* appreciate how forthright she could be.

Sebastian jumped up and put his arm around his wife. "How about you take Harrison to the stables? He hasn't seen the recent changes." He turned to Harrison. "Is that okay with you?"

"I'd rather get the arrangements nailed first," said Harrison.

Sebastian waved an airy arm. "Consider them nailed. Indra is becoming an old hand at weddings now. She helped Lily and Alexander with theirs. And then our first one wasn't very..." He winced as he tried to find the word.

"Romantic?" offered Indra with a laugh. "Fun? Loving? Sociable?"

"All of those things. So that's why we had another one, later, when everything had changed."

"When you'd fallen in love," said Paris.

"Yes," said Indra. "You have the advantage of us there. You're in love already. I can see." She glanced at Harrison and her expression changed. She jumped up. "So, yes, Harrison, why don't we go to the stables? I think you'll be interested in seeing the new horses. We've already had approaches from the US trainers."

His interest in horses tipped the balance. Otherwise he really didn't want to spend time with Indra, who appeared to look straight into his heart and soul and find them both wanting. She was wrong about control being a bad thing. He *could*, and he *would*, control his and Paris's future.

"I won't be long," he said to Paris. She gave him a wan smile and nodded. He looked at Sebastian, who was happily eating a slice of cake and looking for all the world like butter wouldn't melt in his mouth. But he suspected it would. He suspected that his brother and Indra were up to something and he was powerless to stop them. But he'd find out later, no doubt.

CHAPTER 10

Paris watched Harrison leave with Indra, hurt by his apparent indifference to her, and the way her life seemed to be sliding out of control. She'd wanted to be free of control and here she was, like a marionette being pulled by the strings to move in a direction she didn't want to go. It was as if he'd clamped her free will in chains, thwarting any attempt she made to move. She sighed.

"That's a heavy sigh for someone about to have a baby and get married," said Sebastian with a smile, as he brushed away some cake crumbs.

"I think it's quite understated for someone about to have a baby and get married," she replied, with an answering smile. "But, as I'm in company, I thought it preferable to lying on the floor and screaming."

"Like Charlotte, you mean?" said Sebastian. "Yeah, well…" His smile faded. "Change can be pretty scary, but Harrison's a good man. He'll look after you."

She ground her teeth. Sebastian was definitely from

the same mold as Harrison. Both brothers believed she needed looking after. "I can look after myself!"

He held up his hand to pacify her. "Hey, I'm sorry. I didn't mean to suggest you couldn't. It's just that Harrison is such a closed book I thought you might like to know that, deep down—*very* deep down—he's a caring man." He paused as if he were racking his brain to come up with some evidence, knowing that she wouldn't believe him otherwise. His face lit up suddenly, as if he'd thought of something. "He was the only one in the family who used to look after the animals he'd find in the woods." He looked out of the window, his mind obviously far away. "I remember one time, he came bursting into the house furious, tears streaming down his face, holding a dead rabbit." He looked at Paris. "Mother wasn't happy to have blood dripping across the floor. It had been caught in a trap, you see, and Harrison had extricated it."

She frowned as her imagination conjured up the scene. "It doesn't sound like Harrison. Normally he's so self-contained, so..."

"Self-disciplined?"

She nodded.

"He learned to be. We all did. He must have only been around five at the time, right before Mother died. After that, well"—he shrugged—"everything changed."

"How so?"

"Hasn't Harrison told you?"

She shook her head. "He hasn't told me anything about his past."

Sebastian's expression was grim. "No, he wouldn't. He's as bad as me and Alexander. I guess in some ways it was worse for him. We were older and had a certain amount of independence already. But Harrison? He was Mother's baby boy, and she spoiled him rotten." He frowned, as if a sudden thought had struck him. "It must have been harder for him. At least we got time with our mother. He tells me he doesn't even remember her, even though he was old enough to remember."

"I guess he's blocked out the pain," said Paris. It made so much sense now she knew what he'd been through. Once he'd been a sensitive, caring boy but it had been knocked out of him.

Sebastian jumped up and went to the side table where he plucked a photograph from one of the many and walked back to Paris. "Here he is, with Mother." He handed it to her.

"Oh." She gasped at the sight of the boy whose features she recognized, but whose expression she did not. He was looking up at his mother with an open, adoring expression, while she looked back down at him with a fond gaze, her hand around his shoulders. He must have been around three years of age. He had the same dark eyes, shock of hair, and sensuous lips. But this was a different person. This was a person who was open to his emotions. This was the man she'd spent the night with, not the unemotional man she was with now. She'd come to believe that the tender man she'd first met had been an act to seduce her. But here was proof that there was a very different version of Harrison tucked away deep inside, which few people saw.

She handed the picture back to Sebastian. "Thank you for showing me. Without that proof, I'd never have known..."

He replaced the photo back on the table and turned to

her. "Known what a loving heart there is under that chilly, uncommunicative facade?"

She smiled. "Exactly."

"Yes, well. It's there all right. But I'm afraid life with a Richmond brother isn't easy. We are hard nuts to crack." He opened the door. "Come on, let's see what they're doing, shall we? And then we can walk to the church so you can see where you'll be married."

She nodded and followed Sebastian, her heart aching for Harrison—this mysterious man who she'd fallen so hard for.

They walked past the morning room where sunlight, which flowed in through a French window, reflected off the mahogany top of a baby grand piano. A thought occurred to her.

"Did your mother play the piano, like her sister, your Aunt Beth?"

"Mother?" said Sebastian, opening the front door and standing aside for Paris to pass. "Yes, she did. She and Beth were apparently very good."

"Beth's piano at Marsh House is certainly something."

Sebastian turned to her in surprise as they scrunched their way along the gravel path towards the stables. "Beth's piano? No, it won't be hers."

"But Harrison said it *was* hers."

"You must have got the wrong end of the stick. After she got arthritis in her hands, it upset her too much to have the piano there when she couldn't play it, so she got rid of it. No," he said, "there's not been a piano at Marsh House in years."

But, thought Paris as they entered the stables and she watched Harrison stroking the nose of a horse tenderly, there was a piano now. Harrison had bought one for Marsh House for some reason, and the only one she could think of was that he'd got it for her to play. But he was simply too damn proud to tell her. Because if he revealed the kindness and tenderness which she now knew lurked deep in his soul, it meant he was revealing that he had a heart and that he felt something for her.

Bottom line, he had a heart. And that was something with which she could work.

CHAPTER 11

$\mathcal{B}$y the time they reached Blakeney, darkness had fallen and the wind had risen. The gloom was broken only by the street lamps whose pools of light revealed the flint cottages and, at the end of the road, a pub sign which creaked rustily. They took the road which ran along the river, around to the far side of Blakeney. Marsh House stood a shade darker than the navy sky behind it, stolidly resisting the wind as it must have done for over a century.

It looked bleak, it looked forbidding but, Paris realized with surprise, it also looked like a place of refuge.

She glanced at Harrison's shadowy profile. Only seven months ago, her life had been totally different. She'd moved from one secluded place to another, keeping below the radar, shunning company. Always alone. And for him, life had also been very different. It had been lived in a fast lane of polo, parties and people. But then they'd met, drawn together by nothing more than a sense of connection, and made a baby. Their lovemaking had changed their lives and had led them both to here—the northern tip of the Norfolk coast with nothing between them and the North Pole. A fact she knew for sure as she stepped out of the car and shivered, pulling her coat more tightly around her.

Harrison drove the car into the garage and then they walked along the shadowy causeway, which lay between two sets of gleaming mud flats, left by the receding tide.

"I'll have lights put in along here. It's too dangerous as it is," he said.

"I wonder why Beth didn't have them installed?"

Harrison stopped and looked across the marshes. "She once told me she didn't want lights because she liked to look out at the will-o'-the-wisps at night."

"The what?" she asked, thinking she'd imagined things.

"Will-o'-the-wisps. Lights that spring up over the marshes." He leaned in to her. "They say they're the dead spirits come to warn people of something."

She shivered and drew her coat closer. "But... But that's ridiculous."

"They also say," he said, looking into the darkness, "that they're the ghosts of smugglers who died distributing the goods which were landed on the Point."

Despite herself, goosebumps prickled up and down her body, sending chills which had nothing to do with the icy wind, which whipped across her cheeks as she followed his gaze across the flat marshes, devoid of light.

"Smugglers?" she half-whispered.

He looked at her as if alerted by her lowered tone. "For centuries they brought in contraband which had been dropped on the beaches of the Point. They used flat-bottomed boats, coracles or simple barrows to get the goods to cellars all across Norfolk. It was big business. And of course there were deaths. Beth told me the threads of sudden light seen out on the marshes were the souls who couldn't find rest."

"But that's nonsense," she said in another whisper, half-believing it, although she knew it was ridiculous.

"Yes, of course it is. The lights are a chemical phenomenon. Gases released from the marshes." He shrugged. "That's all it is."

"But Beth didn't think so."

"My aunt had a vivid imagination."

She smiled as the picture of his aunt grew ever clearer. Beth had been trying to give her prosaic, lonely nephew a little magic in his life.

It was warm inside the house and once again, Paris was struck by what a different world it was to the outside. She flicked the light switch, and the chandeliers and side lights sprang into life, casting their enchanting glow onto the rich, exotic furnishings. A little bit magical, exactly like the person who'd created it.

She hung up her coat and followed Harrison into the drawing room.

"Care for a drink?" he asked, before grimacing slightly. "I guess not."

"I'll make myself a herbal tea."

In the kitchen, she filled the kettle while looking out at the lights of Blakeney. Harrison was right about one thing. She felt safe here. Safe among the mysterious marsh lights, safe and far away from her father's influence, and held securely within Aunt Beth's magical creation. She smiled and poured the boiling water into a teapot, adding spoonfuls of her favorite herbal tea. She grabbed a cup and took them both into the drawing room.

Harrison stood with his back to the open fire, nursing a brandy, apparently deep in thought. He looked up as she entered.

"Thank you for coming with me to Richmond Manor today," he said a little gruffly, as if embarrassed.

She huffed in surprise as she set down the teapot and cup on the coffee table. "I didn't think I had a choice."

He shot her a slight smile. "You always have a choice."

"Right," she said, taking a seat opposite him. "Except you make it very hard for me to do anything other than what you say."

He shrugged. "Then maybe what I say is the right choice to make."

"For you, maybe."

He shook his head. "For both of us."

He'd seemed distracted ever since they'd left Richmond Manor, as if something had been on his mind. She wondered what it was. Perhaps it had been something Indra had said. Or perhaps it had been revisiting his childhood home, which had unsettled him. Whatever it was, she was grateful, because at least they weren't arguing. And she'd learned things about him, which made arguing the last thing she wanted to do with him.

She tore her gaze away from him and poured a cup of tea, then sat back again, cradling it in her hands. The wind had risen to a light roar as it encircled the house, making one of the sash-cord windows rattle lightly in its frame. She felt another shiver track down her spine. This time it had nothing to do with either cold or fear, and all to do with anticipation.

She was aware of his every movement, every nuance of expression, every sigh. It seemed their one night together had connected her to him in more ways than just their baby. She *felt* him—*knew* him—in the most profound way. The sexual undercurrent that had sparked between them the moment their eyes had met hadn't gone away. It had grown, if anything, and was there now, pulsating with a simmering heat between them. She knew it wouldn't take much to make it flare into a scorching blaze. But did she want to play with fire?

He turned suddenly, and she looked away, scared he'd be able to read her thoughts. And even more scared that he was thinking the same thing. Because then the firestorm would be inevitable.

She swallowed. She couldn't let that happen. He was controlling everything about her. Was he about to control her body, too? She jumped up and walked to the piano, trailing her fingers over its top, needing the soothing comfort she'd always found in it. She reminded herself that he'd bought the piano especially for her. Something he hadn't admitted. What else had he done? What else did he feel for her that he refused to admit either to her or himself?

With the piano acting as a safe barrier between them, she sat on the stool and lifted the lid. Her nostrils flared as she inhaled the smell of polish and dust and felt the ivory keys beneath her fingertips. She pressed her finger on middle C and held it there, the single note ringing out in the room. The sound was accompanied by the whine of the increasing wind and the clattering of the flags on top of the boat masts moored close by.

She looked up into curious eyes, which startled her. It

suddenly felt too intimate, too revealing, to play in front of him. She closed the piano lid quickly.

"Why don't you play?" he asked quietly.

"No, I don't think so."

He tilted his head to one side in query. "Why not?"

"I haven't played for a long time. Not since that night."

"That's a shame. No one could play an instrument that well without loving it," he said, even more quietly still.

She gripped the piano lid as memories flooded her mind.

"Playing the piano saved me," she said at last.

"What from?"

She tossed up in her mind for a few moments before answering. But her defenses were being eroded day by day, minute by minute, and she knew she couldn't hide herself from him anymore. "Hurting myself."

He frowned. "Hurting yourself?" he repeated, clearly baffled. "Why would you do that?"

"Because I was unhappy, Harrison. I wouldn't expect you to understand," she said quickly and defensively before she had time to think. She stopped suddenly. "I'm sorry. I guess that you actually might understand."

"What did Sebastian say to you?"

"Not a lot."

"But enough to make you believe you know me."

She shook her head. "I'm not sure I'll ever know you."

"Good. It's best that way."

She frowned at his response. And then she suddenly understood. He was scared that she'd know him and wouldn't like what she saw there. She knew it instinctively, because she had exactly the same fear. It's what growing up unloved did to you. It made you not even love yourself.

He looked around, as if suddenly restless, as if the spell which had fallen on them as they'd entered the house had been broken somehow. He jumped up and shot her a quick, frowning glance.

"I'm off to bed. I'll see you in the morning. Goodnight."

He walked quickly across the room and was out of the door before she could respond. Paris listened to his retreating footsteps for a while before shifting to the settee and resting her head against its back, looking up at the sparkling lights of the crystal chandelier. What had sent him running? She recalled her last words, that she wasn't sure she'd ever know him. Was he scared she *would* know him, or disappointed that she didn't believe she would? Either way, he couldn't have left more quickly.

And either way, she couldn't shake off her unwanted desire for him. She rested her hands on her thighs and closed her eyes. But it was worse then, because she remembered the feel of Harrison's fingers against her skin, of his lips against hers and other parts of her body. She shivered and sat upright, blinking under the bright lights. No wonder Beth had so many candelabra dotted around the room. She rose, rummaged in the drawers of a sideboard and found some matches. She went around the room, lighting all the candles before switching off the electric lights. The candles flickered as stray gusts of wind found their way through the nooks and crannies of the old house.

She lifted the lid on the piano keys and let her fingers trail over the old ivory keys, slightly yellowed with age. It had been such a long time since she'd played. Impulsively, she softly played a few notes. Her first impression had been accurate. It was in tune and had a lovely tone. Just a few notes, she thought to herself, to see if she could remember anything.

But it seemed she didn't have to remember. As soon as she began, slowly at first, to play the Chopin nocturne, her fingers moved to the correct note, with the correct pressure, one after another, as if with no help from her brain. She picked up the tempo and was soon lost in the nocturne, whose notes seemed to fit the beautiful, comforting and yet eerie solitude of Marsh House.

HARRISON WASN'T sure how long he'd lain on top of the bed, his hands under his head, listening to the poignant notes of first one nocturne, then another, drift upstairs. It took him straight back to his childhood, entranced by his aunt's playing, long after his bed-time. Then, he'd sat at the top of the stairs so he could watch the candlelight flicker and shimmer from the open door, as strains of Chopin, or Debussy or Satie, stirred the deep silence of the house, filling it with beauty and magic. Always French, always romantic, always with a poignant yearning which nearly tore him to pieces.

It was the same now. Except it wasn't his beloved aunt, it was… He hesitated as he strove to find a word to describe Paris. Fiancée sounded clinical, lover was plainly inaccurate. Maybe friend? He huffed sadly. They were the opposite of friends. She was the mother of his child. Pure and simple. He closed his eyes, allowing the notes to flow over and through him. No, it was anything but simple. Then what emotion was it that her notes drove into his very soul, stirring things he didn't think existed?

He jumped up and walked to the window, gripping it as he looked at the black marshes, the trees edging it, bent nearly double following the direction of the wind. Paris hadn't drawn the curtains downstairs. The light from the drawing room poured onto the marshes, mimicking the legendary will-o'-the-wisp with its flickers. She'd lit candles, like Beth used to. He started to move to the door, but thought better of it and sat on the bed. But the music kept on coming. He put his head in his hands and tried to take deep, even breaths, but they became more ragged, more uneven, as if his body insisted that he stop ignoring his connection with this woman—his *need* for her. Every part of him screamed for him to go to her. But still he resisted.

But she didn't make it easy for him. Just as on that first night, the siren call of her music was strong. She revealed herself in the way her fingers touched the keys, lingering a little too long on some, while breaking off in a heart-breaking *staccato* on others, before running down the scales with a *glissando,* which faded to nothing.

Then the music stopped. He opened his eyes to the darkened room. The silence felt shocking after such beauty. He watched as the lights lowered incrementally, as she blew the candles out one by one. Then the marshes were momentarily flooded with light as she switched on the electric light to leave the room. Footsteps echoed in the hallway, and then on each step as they approached, hesitated, and passed his room. He heard her go into her bedroom and shut the door.

He closed his eyes, straining to hear her movements

around her bedroom, which had once been his aunt's. He recognized the creaks of the floorboards he'd used to find so reassuring, exactly as he remembered the squeak and rattle of the sash window as it rose and fell. But not tonight. The window was closed tight against the gusting wind.

But light continued to spill from under the interconnecting door. And he could hear her moving around the room, as if she was as unsettled as he was.

He put his hand on the interconnecting door but withdrew it again. That way lay madness. He backed towards his bed, closing his eyes, trying not to see the light under the door, or sense her presence. He focused on unbuttoning his shirt, tugging it off, and tossing it onto a chair. He slipped his shoes off and sat on the bed, unable to fight his attraction to Paris any longer.

The last of his willpower had evaporated under the onslaught of the music and he found himself opening the door, unable to resist her any longer. He stepped outside onto the landing. The light from her room seeped across the shadowy carpet. He stood there for several seconds, palms flat against the door, absorbing the sense of her. He had no idea what he was going to say to her, or whether she'd turn him away or welcome him. All he knew was that he had to go to her.

CHAPTER 12

He knocked softly on the door. There was the sound of something dropping to the floor, followed by quick footsteps. She opened the door wide. Her dark hair was loose around her shoulders and he recognized the robe she was wearing as one of his aunt's favorites. It was of a deep violet silk, patterned with roses, and beneath it she wore a loose-fitting white, broderie anglaise nightdress.

"Harrison," she said softly, on an exhaled breath. It wasn't a question, but a simple acknowledgement, as if what she'd imagined *would* happen *had* happened. Her voice was as musical as the rest of her. It had mesmerized him the first time he'd heard it, and it mesmerized him now.

"It's late, I know, but..." He tailed off, because how could he describe the reason he was here when there *was* no reason, only simple, compulsive desire?

"But what?"

"I just wanted to..." He had a brainwave. "To remind you that you need to contact Indra tomorrow about the wedding plans." He paused, desperately trying to think up something more plausible.

She gave a smile, which quickly faded, as if she was disappointed with his answer. "Right. Well, thanks." She held onto the side of the door as if she, too, didn't want to close it. It gave him courage.

"I heard you playing. It sounded..." Words failed him to describe how her music had made him feel. He didn't think he'd ever had to describe his feelings before. Why would he, when he didn't think he had any?

She frowned before giving a small, hurt smile. "I guess I'm pretty rusty."

"No!" he said, too emphatically, too awkwardly. "It wasn't that. It's just that it's been a while since I heard you play. But it's different somehow."

"Different? In what way?"

He opened his mouth to speak, but again, words failed him. How could be describe the manner in which she'd played? He didn't do emotion, did he? He shrugged again. "Kind of dreamy."

She smiled and her eyes lingered on his for a few moments, as if she knew he wasn't telling her the whole story. Then the smile widened, and she leaned on the door a little and it opened, revealing a side light with a book open beside it. "I guess I feel kind of dreamy. Like I'm living in a dream."

"So long as it's not a nightmare, I guess it's okay."

"I have to admit, I wasn't sure at the beginning. But now?" She shrugged lightly.

"Now?" he prompted, needing to know what was going on in her mind.

"Now? I've changed my mind."

"And what made you change your mind?" He half-hoped she'd say that *he* had. Male vanity, he guessed.

She frowned. "I'm not sure. A number of things, I guess. Things which made me want to play the piano for the first time in a long time." So much for his ego. "It's wonderful." She breathed in a ragged breath. "It has an exquisite tone."

"Yes, well. My aunt always had the best."

She looked up and held his gaze steadily. She shook her head, and it was his turn to frown at the implicit challenge.

"Your aunt?" she said with a smile. "I don't think so."

"What makes you say that?"

"Sebastian told me she sold her piano when her arthritis got so bad she couldn't play it. Apparently, she was too upset at the sight of it, knowing she couldn't play it any longer." She released her hold on the door and stepped towards him with a new confidence. She came to a halt too close, and after dropping her eyes to his naked chest, she raised them again, and he could see her confidence had grown. "*You* bought this piano. *You* bought this piano for me."

He decided not to deny it. It was clear she knew the truth. But he refused to elaborate, refused to make her realize exactly how much he wanted her to be happy at Marsh House—happy with him.

"Now, why would I do that?"

Her lips tweaked deliciously, and his body responded.

He allowed his gaze to roam over her face, absorbing every little detail of her against which he wanted to press his lips, especially the raised eyebrow.

"You tell me," she said.

"Maybe I'm thinking of my son. Happy mother, happy child."

"Well, you've certainly made me a happy mother. And I've enjoyed playing it, but it's not that which made me happy."

"What then?"

"Figuring you out has made me happy. *And* allowing myself to admit how I feel about you."

It was as if all the air had been sucked out of the room, leaving him breathless. He felt as if he were teetering on a knife's edge, not knowing which way he'd fall. "And what do you feel about me?"

"I understand you a little better now, I think. After going to your childhood home and talking to Sebastian, I feel as if I can almost see the whole of you." She glanced out the window at the three-quarters moon. "Like the moon. Most of it shines brightly, but it's not whole. But I can see the missing part now. Its outline. I know it's there, even if it's hidden."

He hardly understood what she was talking about. All his awareness was focused on her touch. Her hands were flat against his chest while her gaze hadn't left his. Her lips parted as if to say something, but he couldn't wait any longer and dipped his mouth to hers, stealing a kiss from her, stealing the words from her mouth. He was done with words. He leaned in to her and again pressed his lips to hers, half-waiting to see what she'd do, testing her, and satisfying himself at the same time. She gasped, and for a moment he didn't know if she was shocked and going to withdraw, or intensify the kiss. He soon found out.

Her mouth opened under his lips, and he groaned as he stepped closer to her. She melted into him, the swell of her stomach pressing against his body as his tongue found hers. He felt as if he were coming home, and couldn't believe he'd lasted so long without the press of her lips against his, her body against his, and his arms around her, holding her close. It felt so right. How could it have all gone so wrong?

There was no hesitancy now. A barrier had fallen, dropped right away, as her hands smoothed over his chest and around his sides, before coming to rest in the small of his back. She held him close against her. Neither moved, nor made any attempt to pull away from the kiss, which was as tender as it was erotic. The connection which he'd always sensed between them was now made real, and he didn't want it ever to be weakened again. He wanted it strengthened—one kiss, one exploration of the lips, one slide of the tongue at a time.

When eventually they pulled apart, he cupped her face, his fingers glancing over the quickened pulse in her neck. Her breath was coming as fast as his.

"Paris," he gasped, his forehead pressed against hers. "I want you so much."

Her forehead moved against his in agreement.

"I want you, too." She looked up at him with pleading, tearful eyes. "I *need* you, Harrison. I just need you."

He required no further reassurance and, gripping her hand, led her to the bed. He kissed her tenderly and then slid the silky gown from her shoulders. It pooled on the floor. Her long dark hair was loose and curled around her breasts, their shape vague beneath the voluminous white nightdress. He looked at her, perplexed. None of his lovers had ever worn anything so demure.

"How the hell?" He plucked ineffectively at the dress.

She grinned and raised her arms. "Pull it up over my head."

He didn't need telling twice, and he reached down and swept his hands under her nightdress, his palms caressing the backs of her knees and then up her thighs—silky smooth and trembling. Then, with one quick movement, he pulled the nightdress over her head and tossed it to one side. He stepped back so he could admire her. With her eyes slightly hooded, blatantly sexual with her arousal, she looked like a goddess, all sensual curves. He ran his fingertips over her swollen breasts.

"Your breasts," he murmured. "They're so much larger."

"And more sensitive," she said. Her breasts rose and fell quickly. He could see how aroused she was, which made him want to go more slowly to extend her pleasure.

He cupped her swollen stomach. "We must be careful. The baby."

She smiled a secretive smile. "The baby will be fine."

He sucked in a harsh breath, and cupped her breasts before rubbing his thumbs over her fully extended nipples. She gasped, and her face contorted slightly. He stopped immediately.

"Does it hurt?"

Her eyes opened, and she shook her head and smiled. "It's somewhere between pain and intense pleasure. I don't know. All I know is that I don't want you to stop."

He caught her breasts and bent down and kissed each

one. She staggered back a little, and he supported her until she sat on the edge of the bed. He kissed her on the lips before kneeling before her and focusing his attention on her breasts. He took her nipple in his mouth, licked it lightly and, encouraged by her gasp and the way she held his head firm, took it fully into his mouth and suckled gently.

Her breath quickened until it was coming at a fast pant, and her hips jerked under his hands. She'd closed her eyes as if she needed to be alone with the intensity of her feelings. Then suddenly her eyes opened, and she called out his name and her hips bucked against him as she succumbed to an explosive orgasm which rocked right through her.

He swore under his breath, stood up, and quickly undressed. He pulled her to standing, and she leaned against him, his erection pressed against her swollen stomach. He kissed her again, thinking he could never get enough of the taste of her. Their tongues tangled as they devoured each other with all the pent-up frustration created by being separated for too long.

He lowered her onto the bed, and she moved against him instinctively, pleasuring herself as well as him, until even that wasn't enough. She shifted in his arms, pressing her bottom against him, leaving him in no doubt what she wanted.

Grabbing pillows for support, she went on all fours, her breasts brushing the counterpane. He reached out and caressed them before easing himself inside of her, scared he would hurt her. But with each gentle movement, her body moved sensuously against him. He forgot his fears and thrust inside of her, giving her what it was she so clearly wanted. Slowly, like the winding of a clock, the tension increased until it was too taut, and it broke with a cry. He swore and began to withdraw, but she pushed her butt out, forcing him back inside her.

"Are you all right?" he asked.

"Oh my God, yes," she panted, as she rested her head on her forearms. He held her hips as he pulled out and this time pushed gently but firmly into her again. She felt so full and so sensitive. She nearly came with each thrust. Finally, she cried out and he felt her orgasm as her flesh massaged and pulsed around him. In an instant he was there with her, pumping his seed deep inside of her, needing to re-claim her as his woman in the most primitive, most fundamental way. He couldn't let her go again.

He wrapped his arms around her and gently laid her on her side, shifting her hair and kissing her neck. She groaned sleepily, as if all the tension had gone from her and there was nothing left except exhaustion. She snuggled her back and bottom into his body, took one deep sigh and fell asleep against his cock, which was hard again. He could have taken and taken her, could have had sex well into the night and morning and never had enough of her. But she was exhausted. And she was *his* woman, pregnant with *his* child and the complexity of emotions which filled him drove his own impulses down, made them secondary to her wellbeing and comfort. He pressed his smiling lips gently to her hair, so as not to disturb her, and thought to himself that this was a first.

With one arm curled around the top of her head, and the other resting on her hips, he watched over her shoulder as the moon rose higher in the sky, flooding the room with light. Her dark hair gleamed and spread over her naked body. He brushed his lips across her shoulder. It felt like silk. He couldn't believe he'd nearly lost her. He closed his eyes in panic at the thought.

She shivered a little, and he gently removed his hands from her, taking the duvet and laying it over her.

She shifted in her sleep, wriggling into the duvet as if it were a cocoon. And that's all he wanted for her. A cocoon, where he could look after her, make love to her and make sure she had everything she'd always wanted. Where she could be safe. He dropped a kiss gently on her head, snuggling in behind her, and fell asleep.

Paris awoke with a start and looked around. The bed was empty. All there was to show that Harrison had been there the previous night was a dented pillow, a stickiness between her legs, and a pervasive sense of well-being. She sighed and rolled to face where he'd been, stretching out her hand to touch the sheets. They were cold. She glanced at the clock. It was late.

She rolled out of bed, grabbed her robe, and went to the bathroom. It was big and old-fashioned, with its scroll-legged bath and antique fittings, and fitted the house perfectly. She turned on the taps for the bath and then stripped off and caught sight of herself in the mirror. She revolved slowly, forced to admit that she looked more herself again, despite the swollen stomach. She looked... blooming. Maybe, just maybe, life with Harrison wouldn't be a repeat of her parents' marriage. Maybe, just maybe, for once in her life, she was in the right place, at the right time, with the right person.

She smiled at the novel thought as she stepped into the warm bath.

An hour later, bathed and dressed, Paris carefully descended the steep stairs and made her way to the kitchen.

"Good morning, Marie," said Paris cheerfully.

"Good morning!" said Marie, turning to face Paris with a smile. "Well, you're looking much better. You must have slept well."

Paris grin widened. "I did, thank you."

"That's good. Oh, there's a letter for you on the sideboard," Marie said.

Paris's mood altered instantly. "A letter?" A frown tweaked her brow. "But..." She picked up the envelope from the silver tray. Who sent letters anymore? She looked at it for a moment as if it were something poisonous. It was of excellent quality. Thick cream paper with her name and address written in the variable strokes of a fountain pen. Her heart thudded loudly in her ears and she could no longer hear Marie's words. She turned it over and her mouth dried to see the embossed crest in the envelope. She recognized it. She'd seen it every day of her life until she was old enough to leave home.

She interrupted Marie mid-sentence. "When did this arrive?"

Marie continued to stack the breakfast dishes onto the table.

"This morning. I was surprised," she added. "Earlier than the postman usually comes here."

Marie carried on talking, but Paris was no longer listening. She slid her finger along the fold of the envelope and pulled out the letter, unfolding its crisply folded sheets, and quickly checked the signature before scanning its contents.

She sat down, suddenly weak. He knew she was here. Her father knew where she was, and he demanded that she come to him. Or he'd come to her. How the hell did he find out?

CHAPTER 13

$\mathcal{W}$ith a pounding heart, Paris left a puzzled-looking Marie and went in search of Harrison. Marsh House was a large house, but there were only a few places Harrison could be. And Paris went directly to one of them. The library.

She didn't knock but burst into the room, fury fueling her every move. Fury and something else, something much more corrosive—fear.

He jumped up from the desk, which used to be his aunt's—her things now removed to a side table, replaced by a laptop. "What's wrong?" With a couple of strides, he was in front of her. "Is it the baby?"

Trembling, she thrust the letter out in front of her, partly to present it to him, and partly to stop him from advancing any closer. She didn't know whether her anger could withstand his devastating touch, which it had been proved she was helpless to deny.

"No, it's not the baby. He's fine. It's this!"

"What the..." He petered out as he took the letter from

her, looked up at her with a frown, and then withdrew the paper from the envelope, checking first the signature.

"Your father?" His frown deepened. "You've received a letter from your father?"

She crossed her arms above her stomach. "Yes, my father."

He shrugged. "So? What's wrong with that?"

She rolled her eyes. "So many things. First, how the hell did you even *know* the letter was from my father? How did you know his name?"

"It wasn't difficult. After you left, I made enquiries. A lot of enquiries. You hid your traces well from him. He couldn't find you, but I could find him."

"Did you not, for one minute, think that I might have good reason to want to remain hidden from him?"

"Honestly? No, not at first. But then I met him and—"

"You met him?" she spluttered, unprepared for this.

"Yes, of course. Come on, Paris. What did you expect me to do? You and I had one night together—only one night. It wasn't long, but it was enough to know that I wanted you by my side for longer, much longer. And I knew you felt the same way. I knew I hadn't imagined it." He shook his head. "Who could have imagined what we'd shared?"

She licked her lips. "It was sex."

"No," he said, shaking his head again, "It was more than that and I know you're only saying that for your own reasons. I know what it was, and I refused to let you go. So when I found your father, I contacted him."

She pressed her hand against her chest. "What happened?" She could hardly speak the words.

"He agreed to meet me in Zurich."

"You traveled to Switzerland to meet him?" The picture formed in her head—a picture she couldn't bear to imagine.

"Yes," he said warily, watching her expression intently now.

"So you know."

"I know a little."

"I need to know what you know."

"I know he's a powerful man, but little else. He alluded to having some legal issues but said that was all behind him now."

She shook her head in disbelief. "Yeah, right. Once a criminal, always a criminal." She paced across the room, unable to think straight as she felt his eyes follow her. Should she tell him? She had no choice if he wasn't to be suckered into her father's sob story, no doubt designed to get at her. "And it wasn't only that. What he did to my mother and to me. It was..." She bit her lip, unable to go on.

She turned around then. He stood before the desk and window, outlined by the bright morning light. He looked as dominant and as controlling as her father.

He flexed his hands. "It was what?" he asked. "What did he do to you?"

"He killed my mother with his controlling and jealous ways. He forced her to commit suicide."

"Forced?"

"Put it this way. She had no option."

"How old were you?"

"Fifteen. And I've been running from him ever since. And I've succeeded. Until now. Tell me, how did he know I was here?"

He didn't answer immediately. Instead, he scanned the contents of the letter and handed it back to her.

"I told him."

"Why the hell did you do that? You must have guessed I wanted nothing to do with him!"

"I didn't know what had happened between you. And he seemed out of his mind with worry."

She huffed dismissively. "My father can put on a good act."

"I don't know. It seemed pretty genuine to me. So, after I found you here, I let him know you were safe and where you were. It was obvious he cares for you."

"He was putting it on. He hasn't cared for me for a day in his life. He enjoyed having a daughter who he could trot out to friends, have me perform on the piano, before making me disappear again. He only cared for how I could make him appear."

"I think you're underestimating him."

"You don't know who you're dealing with. *I* don't underestimate him. *You* do. I know full well what he's done and what he's capable of doing."

"I can protect you."

She bit her trembling lip as she repeated to herself the words in her father's letter, over and over. "No, you can't."

"Come on, we're here in England. Nothing can happen to you. Besides, I can't believe he'd hurt you."

"He can do anything he wants. He has the power."

She looked out toward the sand dunes which marked the spit of land which sheltered the harbor and creeks and marshes from the North Sea. In the window's reflection, she could see Harrison re-reading the letter a second time, this time more carefully.

He tossed it onto the table. "Answer me one question, Paris. What do you imagine your father wants from this meeting?"

She turned to him. Sunlight streamed through the window onto him. He looked strong, and she wanted to believe him, but he lacked something her father had in abundance—a devious mind.

"He wants control of me and my child. He can't stand anyone walking away. That's why he had my mother's life so tightly controlled after she left once. And that was what drove her to suicide."

"But why would he want control of you?"

She folded her arms trying to keep herself warm, trying to stop herself from shaking, now that the anger had been overtaken by fear. "Because he can. I've seen him play mind games with my mother, just because he could. And, after she died, he tried to do the same with me. He wanted me at home, close to him. He wanted me to marry one of his cronies. Someone he owed a favor to."

"What?"

"He wanted me to marry a man fifteen years older than me with a violent reputation. I was fifteen years old, and he was going to marry me off as soon as I turned sixteen. I had to leave, and I had to cut all ties. Otherwise, I knew I'd end up the same as my mother, with the same eating disorder and with the same bleak, unhappy future. He hasn't changed, whatever he said to you. He's always been the same. I know what he's like. You don't."

He stepped towards her and gripped her arms. "I won't allow him to control you."

"No," she said, "I don't suppose you would. Because you're as bad as he is, aren't you?" She glanced at his hands, which gripped her arms. "You want to control me, to keep me for yourself." She shook her head. "I can't be that woman, Harrison. I simply can't."

He released his hold on her and stepped away abruptly. "That's not what I want."

"Isn't it?"

"No, and you have to believe me," he said.

"I believe that's what *you* believe. But you've shown me nothing to make me think different. Nothing to make me trust you."

"You must trust me."

"How can I?"

He shrugged. "How can you not? Was last night nothing? You're expecting my baby and we have to face our future together. There is only you and me, and our child. Whatever you're afraid of, we'll face head on and sort it out."

She shook her head. He was wrong. But, despite that, she couldn't help feeling relieved, despite believing him to be quite wrong.

"I met your father in a hotel in Zurich. I know his name and I sensed that he was powerful because the hotel appeared to be his office. But I don't know why he is so powerful."

She sucked in a deep breath. Harrison knew so much and she knew that not withholding the last piece of information might make him see what he was up against.

"My father is Luis Caparelli. That you already know. What you probably don't know is my father is head of the Napoli mafia."

His eyes widened in shock.

"Your *father* is? I had no idea."

"You wouldn't. No one outside the mafia or law enforcement would. He makes sure of it. Harrison, there's no stopping my father when he wants something. And he wants me and, when he discovers I'm pregnant, he'll come for my child."

"*Our* child. And he knows you're pregnant. I told him."

Sick with fear, she pushed past him.

"Paris! You can't keep running forever. It's time to face him, and I'll be with you this time."

She paused and closed her eyes tight against the fear which gripped her. "I can't do it."

"You can. I know you can. There is no other way. You have to see that."

She continued into the hall, where she grabbed her coat and stumbled outside onto the path. She glanced towards the village and immediately struck out on the path through the marshes. Every instinct inside of her screamed to get away—from the village, from her father and from Harrison—from everyone who wanted a part of her and her child.

CHAPTER 14

*H*arrison watched her leave. She walked quickly, her gaze darting back and forth as if she expected her father to jump up from the marshes and grab her. She hesitated once, scanned the town and then turned her back on it and continued along the raised pathway which led toward the sandbank and the sea beyond.

He understood her now. Things which he couldn't figure out slotted into place. She'd had her faith in her father destroyed at an early age and he'd formed a threatening shadow over her life ever since. Her only response had been to hide. He should have trusted in her. He shouldn't have dismissed her fears as nonsense. Because they weren't. And it was up to him to make things right. To protect her and his child. And he would, even if he died doing it.

While his first impulse was to run after her and bring her home, he knew he had to act differently now. He knew he had to sort out this mess and allow her some space.

He went to the library and picked up the phone. He had some calls to make. He had security to arrange.

THE WIND WHIPPED her hair as she looked around. She was alone and yet she felt safe here. The long walk to the sandbank had worn off some of her agitation. Although it was winter, the sun shone clear, making the mud flats gleam and the gold grasses ripple brightly in the breeze.

She'd walked as far as she could and now a branch of the river blocked her from Blakeney Point—a sandbank which sheltered Blakeney from the force of the North Sea —and she could go no further. But she wanted to. She looked out across the river, beyond the sandbank to the brilliant, cold blue of the sea, and found relief in that emptiness, that solitary condition in which she could find comfort. Then her eyes lowered to the Blakeney Eye, now a small island in the river channel, and spotted the depression and tumble of stones which showed the remains of the old chapel. In medieval times, when the river channel had taken large ships to the neighboring town of Cley, monks had taken a toll on everything passing by. Always money, driving the world. She hated it. It had been the downfall of her mother and at the root of her father's vice.

"Paris!"

Her name came to her on a gust of wind. Startled, she looked around. Harrison was striding towards her, hair ruffled, concern etched on his face. Even as the need to escape his control arose, so did an appreciation that he hadn't let her disappear into the marshes alone on a winter's morning. She knew if she strayed off the path, the marshes could prove lethal. So she simply sighed and shot him a smile. It was hardly his fault that her father was a crook, hell-bent on tracking her down.

He reached out for her hand as he approached her, clenching it, and pulling her into his arms. She was engulfed by his warmth and strength and for a moment she leaned into him, as if it were the safest place in the world. But she knew it wasn't, nowhere was, and eventually she pulled away with a sad smile.

"I'm so sorry, Paris," he said, as he searched her face, as if desperately trying to find traces of forgiveness in her. Could she? He'd brought to her doorstep the man from whom she'd been running her whole adult life.

She struggled but couldn't get out of her mind that Harrison, despite her feelings for him, was as controlling as her father.

"I know and I understand," she said, taking a step backward. "But I'm scared. You don't know what he's like. You don't know what he's done."

"I'll protect you. I have security people coming twenty four hours a day, seven days a week. You'll be safe, I promise you."

She shook her head again. "No. That would drive me crazy."

"I don't understand."

"I'm not surprised. I hardly understand myself, but I know two things."

"What are they?"

"One, no security, and two, I have to face up to this. I can't run my whole life. You made me see that."

"You mean you'll take up your father's invitation and go see him?"

She heaved a big sigh. "I guess. I think I've reached the end of the road." She tapped her stomach. "Luca needs to be born into a world where his mother isn't hiding from anybody. I want him to take his first steps with a free heart. Not scared of his own shadow, like I've been most of my life."

"Good. It's the only way. When shall we go?"

"I don't know. Not yet. After Luca is born." She looked up at him uncertainly. It was one thing to decide to face her father, it was another to do it.

"Sooner would be better."

"No, not yet. I'm not ready. I'll be better able to cope when I'm not pregnant."

"You won't have to cope alone."

She shook her head. "No, this is something I need to do by myself."

He raised a determined eyebrow. "There is no way I'll allow you to go by yourself."

"Allow? Harrison! I'm a grown woman. If I want to see my father by myself, I will. And you do *not* decide what I should do!"

He shrugged. "But your father isn't just any father, is he? You can't go alone. Surely you see that?"

She chewed her lip, indecisive for a few moments, before nodding. She would like him to be there with her. Because, whatever their issues and problems, she knew that he'd do his utmost to protect her, and Luca, from her father.

She sighed. "Okay. I will *allow* you to come." She shot him a dark look. They'd have that conversation later.

"Good. So what will you tell him?"

"That he doesn't have any hold on me anymore. I'm no longer fifteen, but a grown woman with a life of my own."

"And he can hardly marry you off if you're already married."

"You don't know what my father is capable of."

The expression on Harrison's face changed, and she realized that now he probably did. A muscle in his jaw flickered. "We'll be safe. I'll bring security with me. Nothing will happen to either of us."

"Only if you don't bring security. That would be asking for trouble, believe me."

"I guess you know best. So no security. When shall we see him?"

"Soon. Not yet. I need a little time. I still think it would be best to see him after we're married. I'll feel so much safer then."

"Okay. If it makes you feel better, and it's only a few weeks away. We'll leave it until then. Now," he said, grimacing as he glanced up at the sun over which a cloud had slid, lowering the temperature immediately. Paris shivered. "How about we go home and make all the arrangements?"

"It won't be happy families, I'm afraid."

She fell into step beside him, putting her hand through his offered arm, glad of his support. She'd walked further than she'd meant to.

"Yeah, well, I'm not exactly used to happy families, am I?"

They walked a few paces, and she wondered if he was going to elaborate.

"Why aren't you? What happened?"

"Now that, Paris, is a long story."

"Well, it's a long walk ahead of us." She searched his face, wondering if he would drop the mask behind which he hid so much from her. He exhaled heavily and nodded.

"True." He pulled her to him in a brief hug. "Are you ready?"

She smiled. "I'm ready."

By the time they reached Marsh House, Paris understood what had made Harrison the man he was. A father devastated by the premature death of his wife, three brothers deprived of his love and damaged by his cruel indifference.

He opened the door to Marsh House for her and she hesitated, touching the lapel of his coat with her palm. "And yet Sebastian and Indra believe your father brought them together."

"There's no doubt about it. He did."

"And Alexander believes your father wanted him to meet Lily."

"Yep. Again, Lily's contract was iron clad. There was no other way of interpreting it. Our father wanted Lily's big heart to work on Alexander. And it did."

"So, I wonder what your father has done for you?"

He gritted his teeth firmly and his eyes went cold. "Nothing. That much is clear. My brothers reckon I was saved the worst of it, being the youngest. But at least they have memories of our mother. I have none."

"But you have memories of your aunt—Aunt Beth.

That relationship must have been the most important one in your life."

He nodded.

"Maybe your father didn't need to do something posthumously. Maybe he helped you before he died by encouraging your relationship with Beth. Maybe he did leave a legacy for you, one that showed you love and support when you needed it most. And then there is the inheritance he left you. You said it required you to spend more time in Norfolk, the one place you resisted coming to. Maybe he wanted you to stop drifting around the world and settle down and face up to the things you'd been running from for so long."

As he helped Paris off with her coat and watched as Marie fussed over her, Harrison thought about what Paris had said. Was she right? Had his father felt that he'd already provided someone for him who had helped him through life? If it was true, then he'd certainly had the advantage on his brothers, in that Beth had been there for him until only recently.

And the inheritance? It was true that there had been a stipulation upon his inheritance that he spend most of his time in Norfolk for the first two years, a stipulation he'd successfully managed to ignore. At first, it merely seemed curious and annoying. Something his father, who knew Harrison avoided the county of his birth, had done to annoy him from beyond the grave. But what if it wasn't about annoyance? What if it was about reparation?

He stood by the door, watching Paris for a few moments—her expressive features, the light upon her face

—like a man deprived. He didn't think he'd ever get enough of her. Their love-making proved that. Simply being with her proved that. But he knew she wanted something more—something he couldn't give her. Whatever his father had or hadn't done, he knew he had all he wanted in Paris. If only she could accept the fact that his heart wasn't whole and that love would never be a part of the picture. If only.

CHAPTER 15

*P*aris couldn't believe how quickly the day of her wedding had arrived.

At first, the date had seemed too distant to contemplate. Between worrying about her father, trying to figure out a new life with Harrison and, all the while, pre-occupied with her pregnancy, she'd hardly given the wedding a thought. But the days had slid by, one lazy day at a time. She didn't think she'd ever slept so much, or done so little, in her life. Between walking on the marshes with Harrison or shopping in the local town in the morning, afternoons spent dozing in front of the open fire at Marsh House, and nights of passionate lovemaking, Paris felt rested and refreshed, like she'd never felt before.

When she'd been on her own, she'd always been working to supplement the inheritance she'd received from her mother—either as a waitress or earning a few more dollars by playing the piano. And all the time, she'd been watchful. Jumping at the sound of an Italian accent, prepared to run if someone so much as touched her arm or shoulder, or looked at her for a few moments too intensely. She realized now that she'd been living on her nerves, and the relief of not having to live life like that any longer was huge. It only confirmed her decision that she had to see her father again. The phase of her life when she'd lived in fear was over. It had changed the minute she'd met Harrison in the Caribbean. And changed again when he'd turned up on her doorstep in Blakeney. She'd thought at the time it had changed for the worse, but now? She felt almost content. *Almost.*

There was one thing lacking, one question mark over her happiness. Harrison never told her he loved her. Never told her he had feelings for her. She sensed he did. She *believed* he did. But in her darker moments, she was forced to admit that it was a guess, and the truth could be very far from her guess. Was this marriage simply a way to keep his child with him, as he'd said at first? Or was it something more? Either way, it cast a shadow over her happiness. A shadow she hoped wouldn't darken further and resemble her parents' poisonous relationship once they were married.

But today wasn't going to be one of those darker days. It was her wedding day, and the grounds of Richmond Manor had put on a sparkling display on this cold, bright morning. Through the French windows of the drawing room, where she and Indra and Lily were gathered, she had a clear view of the entire front sweep of the manor's grounds. The frost glittered in the sunshine beneath the bare-limbed branches of the trees.

She felt a hand on her shoulder, and she turned to see Harrison searching her face.

"What are you doing here?" she squeaked, glancing at

her soon to be sisters-in-law, who hadn't noticed Harrison's entrance.

He grinned. "Checking up on you. Are you okay?"

"Yes, I feel great." She rolled onto her tiptoes and kissed him, and raised an eyebrow. "How do you feel?"

He nuzzled into her neck. "Like we should go back to bed."

She laughed and leaned her cheek against his chest. "Time for that later."

"Yes, indeedy!" called Lily, clamping one firm hand on Harrison's shoulder. "Much later. You shouldn't even be catching a *glimpse* of your fiancée before the ceremony."

"I hardly think we're going the conventional route."

Lily shrugged. "All the more reason to begin now."

"What's the point?"

"The point is, you'll see your beautiful bride afresh as she joins you at the altar. She'll be like a new person and you can fall in love all over again."

Harrison's smile dropped, and he excused himself. Paris moved away, not wanting Lily to see the shadow which had passed over her face.

"What's got into him?" asked Lily, always one to speak her mind.

Paris pasted on a smile and looked at Lily with a shrug. "Who knows? Wedding day jitters, I guess."

Lily rolled her eyes as she passed a glass of sparkling juice to Paris. "Men! They make out they're so macho and brave to the outside world but, when they're alone with you..." She shrugged. "You know what I mean, eh?"

Paris huffed a surprised laugh and nodded.

Lily looked back to see Alexander and Sebastian enter the room and join Harrison. "Talking of men." She shook her head. "They're not doing what they've been told. Oi!" she shouted. "You guys shouldn't be here."

Alexander blithely ignored her, finished pouring a second glass of champagne, and brought the two glasses over. He didn't bother to dispute her comment, but handed her a glass, tipped her chin with his fingers and kissed her lips. After he moved away, Lily's indignant expression had been replaced by an adoring look which had obviously wiped away any thought of telling the men to leave.

"Paris, you look beautiful," said Alexander, with the legendary smooth-talking charm which his brother didn't share.

"Thanks to Lily and Indra. Lily found this dress." She smoothed down the empire line gown. The pearl detail in the bodice took away the focus from her baby bump over which the ivory silk skimmed. Paris's thanks were heartfelt, because she really didn't know what she'd have done without Lily, whose big personality made up for the lack of people, and Indra, whose sensitive nature had ensured Paris felt like it was her special day.

"My wife has immaculate taste." He shot her a cheeky grin. "After all, she chose me, didn't she?"

Lily pretended to growl. "Come here, you."

Alexander didn't need to be told twice and was captured by his wife's arms.

"It's true, isn't it?" he said confidently.

"Because I love you," she said with a softening smile.

"I love you, too," responded Alexander, before kissing her with a kiss which was quite different to their previous one. This one was gentle and loving—proof of their words.

After they pulled away, Paris caught Harrison's gaze and she wondered if he was thinking the same as her. Wondering whether Harrison could ever love Paris as Alexander loved Lily. His swift glance away suggested that, whatever he was thinking, he was uncomfortable with the display of love.

But where did that leave her? She shivered, and Indra noticed.

"Come over here," said Indra. "Come closer to the fire."

Paris did as Indra suggested. The log fire was blazing in its huge hearth and Paris was glad of its heat, because she did suddenly feel cold—the chill of wondering whether a loveless marriage of convenience was all that lay ahead of her. Sure, the sex was great, and sure, Harrison controlled everything to make sure her life was as easy as possible. But the chill of uncertainty still lingered in her heart.

"You're not still cold, are you?" asked Lily with concern.

Sebastian glanced out the window. "Hope you've got something warm to wear to the church. It's not exactly balmy weather out there."

"I'm fine, really. Just feeling"—she shrugged—"a little weird. And I have Lily's glorious white fur coat to wear to the church." The women exchanged grins. They'd grown closer as they'd worked on the wedding arrangements. Not that there had been many. It would be a family affair. But Paris really didn't want anything bigger. And it seemed Indra, given her past, understood completely without her having to explain further.

They all gathered around the log fire in the sitting room. Paris had asked that they wear white. Lily's usual sexy attire was a shade more demure in the fine woolen dress she wore, although it still enhanced her amazing figure. If Lily hadn't been such a lovely person, Paris had to admit she might have felt a little frumpy, being so heavily pregnant, and a lot envious of her and Alexander's happiness. And Indra looked every inch the elegant lady of the manor, dressed in a white trouser suit with satin lapels and white carnation in her buttonhole.

"I think a toast is in order," said Sebastian, who, as the eldest brother, ably assumed the role of host for the occasion. He turned to the others and raised his voice. "Ladies and gentleman, let's raise our glasses and drink a toast to the happiness of Harrison and Paris. May their future be filled with good health, happiness and lots of babies," he said, with a sly grin in Indra's direction.

"And love," added Indra. "Don't forget love." She smiled encouragingly at Harrison and then at Paris. Harrison didn't seem to notice, and Paris looked away, unable to give Indra more than a ghost of a smile.

But the moment passed, as Lily regaled them all with anecdotes of her and Alexander's wedding.

Harrison stayed by her side but, unlike before, they didn't touch each other. Something had changed. In the run up to the wedding, they'd been physically close, but now a bus could have driven between them without causing harm. Maybe it was all this talk of love. Maybe he was regretting the wedding. Maybe all he wanted was to walk away and keep walking back to his old life. She had no idea, because he refused to talk about his feelings, his thoughts, or his hopes. He was so macho and closed off from his feelings, it was painful.

And inside, her heart was aching and all she could do

was focus on not giving way to the heartache she felt, not allowing the tears to flow. That could come later. When no one was watching. She felt so heavy and tired now. She made her excuses and sat down. Indra pushed a footstool towards her.

"May as well make yourself comfortable now. You'll be on your feet once we get to the church."

Paris nodded, scared to speak because she wasn't sure what would emerge.

Indra frowned. "Are you all right?" she asked.

"Yes, just..." She blinked back the tears, but was saved from answering by an eruption of laughter after Lily gave the punchline to a joke. The joke was obviously pretty close to the knuckle because the men were all laughing. All except Harrison, who looked at Paris. She was grateful for any sign of attention and smiled at him tentatively. His lips lifted at the corner, but there was still a sadness in his eyes. He put down his half-finished drink and looked out the window.

"Looks like the cars are here," he said.

CHAPTER 16

The morning sun shone low through the frozen branches and snow of the woods, creating magical beams of splintered light. It was only a short walk to the church, but given Paris's advanced pregnancy and the light layer of snow which had frozen on the ground, it had been decided to drive there. The original plan of separate cars for the men had been scrapped. There hardly seemed any point when they were all mingling freely with each other.

For all the beauty of the morning, and Indra's care, Paris felt frozen on the inside, too. It was clear all Harrison was doing was going through the motions so that he could make sure he had control of his son, like he had control of her. As a polo player he'd been famous for two things—his cold heart and expert control of his horse—and she felt as if she were being subjected to the same treatment: manipulated and cajoled to his will until she didn't even realize it.

She glanced at Harrison. He looked as handsome as

ever in his tux, but with an expression which appeared to fool everyone except her. Only she could see the tension around his mouth. He dispensed with the driver and she slipped into the front seat next to him.

"You don't have to go through with this, even now, if you don't wish to," she said.

He looked at her, and she felt it was the first time he'd really looked. Then he looked back at the narrow lane which took them to the church, a longer route than by foot.

"I want to get married. You know I do."

"You want to own me and our son, that's all I know."

"Don't be ridiculous. No one owns anyone."

Heat rose through her, burning the sadness away, like the sun was beginning to melt the snow on the branches.

"So I'm being ridiculous now, am I?"

"Frankly, yes. You agreed to this marriage, so I think there's little point in talking about backing out of it!"

"Excuse me! It wasn't me who was sitting in the living room, refusing to talk to anyone. It wasn't me who looked as if I was going to a funeral and it wasn't me who couldn't even bring yourself to look at your future wife." Her voice choked on the last few words. She looked out the window once more. They were on the main road, which would take them around a circuitous route to the church. She swiped away a tear, not caring whether her make-up was smudged. No doubt her sisters-in-law to be would imagine they were tears of joy. And, equally no doubt, neither of Harrison's brothers would notice because they were oblivious to everything except their own women. Shame Harrison didn't take a leaf out of their books.

"Of course I could look at you. I'm looking at you now, aren't I?" he said, glancing at her briefly before focusing back on the road.

"You don't want to marry me, any more than I want to marry you. And that's the truth of it."

"It's a means to an end. That's all. Nothing more."

She was silent.

"Come on, Paris! It's nothing. It's simply something we have to do for our child. That's all."

"That's not marriage," she said in a low voice.

"Yes, of course it is."

"No, it's not. And you can't tell me you ever imagined it would be like this."

He gave a heavy sigh. "I can't say I've ever imagined it."

"No, I'm sure you didn't."

A heavy silence fell as they turned up the tree-lined avenue which led to the church. The picture-perfect winter scene seemed to mock her.

"Okay, so tell me how you imagined it," he said at last.

"You want to know?" she said, unable to stop the tears from streaming down her face. She had his undivided attention now as he pulled up outside the church. The other car pulled up behind them, and the sound of laughter and chatter filled the frigid air. "You want to know what I'd always imagined a wedding to be like?"

"Sure. Tell me," he said. She hated how off-hand he sounded.

"I'd always imagined it would be perfect."

"Perfect only happens in the movies."

"You're wrong." She looked out through her tears at the other two couples. "Look at them. They've found perfect. There's love there, in their hearts—you can see it shining through. And it's that which makes it perfect."

He made a scoffing sound.

"You can hide behind that facade all you like, Harrison Richmond! You can pretend you have no feelings, but I know otherwise. You *do* have them. I'm just sad that you don't have them for me."

With that, she swiped away her tears with a handkerchief she plucked out of the pocket of the fur coat and blew her nose. She shot a watery smile at Sebastian and Alexander, who stood waiting for Harrison. Sebastian opened the door for her and Lily and Indra helped her out of the car. The driver's car door banged shut, loud in the clear air, and Harrison walked around, joining the men who disappeared into the church.

Accompanied by Lily and Indra, Paris walked through the fine layer of icy snow, following the melting steps left by the men.

"Are you sure you're okay?" asked Lily.

Paris nodded.

"Come here," said Lily, with sympathy in her voice, giving her a hug. "These damned men are worth it in the end, but they sure know how to turn a girl's life upside down." Lily took a tissue from her bag, and gently tilted Paris's face upward to wipe away the smudges of mascara from her cheek.

"Just as well you don't need make-up," said Indra with a sad smile.

"It's those Italian genes," said Lily. "You'll be gorgeous when you're a great grand-nonna."

"Ha!" said Paris, cheered by these two strong women who, she knew, had both gone through a lot to achieve their happy marriages. She tapped her stomach. "I have to get Luca out first. I can't imagine having a baby boy, let alone a grown man with children of his own."

"One step at a time," said Indra, resting her head against Paris's.

"It *will* happen," said Lily, her bravado dropping for once, revealing the tender heart she hid inside. "And then, all of this will seem like a long-distant dream. You won't even be able to remember what the tears were for because your heart will be full of love."

Paris gave a brave smile and looked away. She couldn't bring herself to tell Lily that it was already full of love—for Harrison, and for her unborn child. But it was aching for the lack of being loved.

"Now," said Indra, handing Paris her bunch of spring flowers which had been picked from the manor house's orangerie. "Are you ready?"

"Yes." She turned to them both. "And thank you. I've never had close women friends and you two are—" She stopped abruptly as more tears threatened.

The two women cried out in unison. "No need to thank us," said Lily firmly. "You can do that in the future when we have family get-togethers. Now you need to focus on you and Harrison, and getting married."

Indra gave her another hug. "Sometimes the marriage comes first and the love after."

"I hope you're right," said Paris, facing the church in which her future husband waited.

Paris walked up the aisle of the ancient church, her low pumps skimming over the worn stone of the nave as she approached Harrison and his brothers, both of whom were best men. Sebastian looked serious, Alexander was smiling and Harrison… Harrison's frown hid a myriad of things.

They'd purposely kept their vows to a minimum. When they'd discussed it, Harrison said he didn't have anything to say that couldn't be expressed by the usual vows. So Paris hadn't told him the words she'd wanted to say, knowing that he wouldn't want to hear them. So, awkwardly, they'd gone with the words in the guide the vicar had given them. And now she repeated the words after the vicar, taking Harrison Richmond to be her legal husband.

But, to her surprise, the vicar didn't continue with the rote words to Harrison. Instead, the vicar nodded encouragingly at Harrison, who looked strangely nervous.

"Paris," he eventually said in a hoarse, emotional voice. "I have something to say."

There was a collective gasp. He wasn't meant to be saying anything like this. He gripped her hands more tightly and all she could do was stare, open-mouthed, at him, terrified at what she was about to hear. Was he going to call the whole thing off? Tell her it was all a terrible mistake, that they should live separate lives and share custody of their baby? What the hell? The pause was interminable.

"Harrison!"

Sebastian gave Harrison a sharp shove. "Get on with it, man," he said under his breath.

Harrison took a deep breath. "Paris, I'm sorry, but this is hard for me to do."

Paris felt sick and the room swayed a little. His grip on her tightened.

"Tell me," she said.

"We talked about special vows and I said I didn't have any. But I lied. I do have things to say to you. Your music led me to you. I knew you through it. And from the moment I saw you, I felt something." He shrugged. "Felt something stir inside of me, and I knew that we were meant to be together."

She wasn't sure if she'd heard right. "Something stirred?"

He nodded, as if he was relieved she'd understood. She hadn't.

"And we'll be good together, I'm sure of it." She'd have believed him more if he hadn't pumped her hands as if he were trying to convince himself.

There was a long pause, and she realized that he'd finished. One thing for sure was that her new husband wasn't good with words.

"Right," she said, unsure how to respond.

She was saved by saying anything further by the vicar clearing his throat and continuing with the brief ceremony.

The ring was slipped on her finger, the vicar's words unheard, as Paris gazed into Harrison's eyes, which held a relief she didn't share—as if he was satisfied he'd said what he had to say. Her mind re-ran his words, trying to find a saving grace in them and failing. Suddenly the ceremony was over and the organ began to play.

Sebastian huffed a stifled laugh and clapped Harrison on the back. "And I thought I was bad!" he said, his words barely heard over the strident notes of the organ.

Feeling numb, Paris met Indra's sympathetic gaze. Lily sighed, shook her head, as if in despair, and turned away with a raised eyebrow at Alexander. Alexander leaned over Harrison's shoulder. "Five out of ten, brother. Needs work." Harrison frowned.

With Harrison frowning and Paris fixing an uncertain smile on her face, they walked down the aisle to the sound of the organ blasting out the wedding march and bells ringing. Paris's heart sank even further as they stepped into the decorative south porch with its pillars sweeping up into an ornate arch. A photographer, no doubt organized by Indra, stopped them there. Paris kept a smile on her face as she stood on the worn stone, created by the feet of countless generations of the Richmond family and villagers, and wished she were anywhere else.

As the photographer organized them into different groups, Paris wondered if she'd ever have the courage to look at the photographs, knowing the mixed emotions which filled her. She doubted it. Eventually, the photographer was satisfied, and the three brothers stepped forward, glad to be released.

"Okay?" asked Indra with a sympathetic smile.

"Sure."

"You did well, considering."

Paris gave a small laugh. She knew Indra was referring to her pregnancy. But she felt she'd done well considering Harrison's botched attempt at saying something heartfelt. How could you say something from the heart when it was patently clear he didn't have one?

She shivered as she stepped out from the shelter of the porch. Lily slipped the floor-length white fur coat around Paris.

"Thank you," said Paris, grateful for the support of these two women.

"You're welcome," said Lily, giving her shoulders a squeeze

She looked beyond the photographer, to the trees which surrounded the church. Snow had begun to fall again and was settling on their bare branches, vivid white against the slate-gray sky. It was beautiful, but frozen and cold. It seemed fitting somehow.

"I hope it improves," said Lily, looking up at the snow-laden sky with a frown.

"So do I," said Paris, looking directly at her husband.

CHAPTER 17

*B*ut the weather didn't improve.

After they'd eaten a sumptuous lunch, all six of them returned to the drawing room—tired and a little subdued. Indra ushered Paris into an easy chair by the fire and insisted she put her feet up on a tapestried footstool. Paris glanced through the window at a world of white. The snow had continued to fall, its dense flakes settling and coalescing with others, creating small drifts against the trees. Paris imagined standing outside, arms stretched to the falling snow, feeling its cold kiss on her limbs before seeping into her aching heart. But she didn't need to imagine how numb she would feel. She felt that already.

"Indra said you might enjoy this." She turned to find Harrison standing in front of her, offering her a warm drink. Harrison gave an awkward grimace. "The others are still on champagne, but she thought you might enjoy something more warming."

Paris gave a soft, amused grunt, as she couldn't help

thinking being married to Indra would be a lot easier than being married to Harrison. At least during the day. At night… She looked up at the tall, incredibly handsome man she'd just married and remembered their passionate nights together. At night Harrison was exactly the man she wanted.

"Thank you," she said, sitting up with a smile. It had been awkward ever since that moment in the church when Harrison had more or less told the world that he didn't love her but wanted to be with her despite that. As declarations went, it wasn't the best. "Indra's spot on." She took a sip of the creamy hot chocolate and wondered why Harrison was frowning at his brothers. He looked back at her, shaking his head as if completely baffled.

"What's got into everyone?" Harrison said at last. "My brothers are making fun of me. Indra's treating me like I'm not well, and Lily is cross with me. What have I done?"

"Do you really not know?" she asked.

"I wouldn't ask if I did."

"Your vows, Harrison, they were…" She shook her head as she tried to express how awful they were.

"Bad," he said with a sigh, his gaze fixed to the floor. "Terrible, weren't they?"

She nodded.

He reached out for her hand. "Hey, I'm sorry. I told you I'm hopeless with words."

"That wasn't the problem," she said, glancing out the window. "I think we should go soon," she said before he could respond. She really didn't want to hear again how much he didn't love her. "If we leave it any longer, we may have trouble getting home."

He smiled. "I like that you think of it as home."

"Yes, I guess I do. Which is even more surprising because home is meant to be where the heart is. Ironic, really."

He was silent for a few moments. Then he took her hands in his. "I'm sorry. It's me. You've married a cold man. It's who I am."

"But that's not the problem. Because I know you're not cold. I've seen your heart in action and I know you feel things. It's just…"

"Just what?"

"It's just not there for me. That's what makes me sad. Not your lack of words, not your lack of heart, but your lack of love for me."

She gripped the sides of the chair and pushed herself to standing.

"Are you two off now?" asked Lily.

Sebastian checked the weather. "Probably a good idea. Hope it clears for your flight."

She frowned and shot Harrison a questioning look. She really didn't want to acknowledge openly that she had no idea that a flight was booked, no idea that Harrison had planned a trip, and no idea if it included her or not. Harrison didn't meet her gaze, which didn't bode well. Instead, he got up.

"The forecast is fine over Stansted."

Her knowledge about what lay ahead had just doubled —a flight from Stansted Airport.

The women embraced Paris with warm wishes for her trip. Paris kept her smile fixed on her face, hoping it wouldn't fade before she got into the car. She knew she'd found good friends in Indra and Lily, and also knew she couldn't have got through the wedding without either their organizational help or their emotional support. And she had mixed feelings about leaving them. On one hand, she'd miss their uncomplicated understanding and support but, on the other, she wouldn't have to pretend that her marriage was perfect. Although she suspected they already knew that.

The farewells outside the manor were brief as the snow was falling faster now and, with a sense of relief, they drove off. Paris gave Harrison the opportunity to tell her where they were going. But he said nothing. Then she gave him a little longer, waiting until they reached the main road. Still nothing.

"Harrison, are you going to tell me where we're going?"

He grinned, and she couldn't believe how delighted he looked.

"It's a surprise."

"I don't like surprises. You might not know me well, but I'd have thought you'd figured that one out."

His smile fell a little. "Seb and Alex reckoned women liked surprises."

"Their women might. Did you ask Indra or Lily?"

He shook his head.

"Right. If you had, they might have better informed you. So, where are we going?"

"We're going on our honeymoon."

"You've never mentioned anything before about a honeymoon."

"Well, I am now."

She bit her lip, trying to hold back her fury. This topped everything. Not only didn't he love her, but he couldn't even be bothered to share with her he'd organized a honeymoon.

"When were you going to tell me?"

"When you noticed we weren't returning to Marsh House." He glanced at her as he drove carefully along the snow-filled lanes away from the coast. "I thought you might like the surprise. But I guess Seb's comments gave it away."

She heaved a deep sigh. "I've had enough surprises for a lifetime. All I want is to go back to Marsh House."

He was silent as he continued driving *away* from Marsh House. "Aren't you interested in what I want?" she continued.

"I'm interested in what you need," he answered carefully.

"And you believe you know me better than myself, I suppose."

He glanced at her. "In this case, yes."

"And what case would this be?"

He paused before answering. She didn't like it when he did this. It meant he was carefully concocting an answer. It meant he had something to hide.

"We're married. It's usual to have a honeymoon. I thought you'd be pleased."

"I'm heavily pregnant, Harrison. Most airlines wouldn't want me aboard."

"We're not traveling on most airlines. I've asked a favor of a friend. His Lear jet is at our disposal and we're not going far."

"Where are we going?"

"Now that is a secret I'm going to keep for a little while longer."

Paris sat back in the car. It seemed she wasn't going to get anything further from her new husband. So she might as well sit back and wait.

There were some things money *could* buy, thought Paris lazily, as she stretched out on the bed in the luxurious cabin of the Lear Jet cruising at 35,000 feet above somewhere in Europe. And comfortable travel was at the top of the list.

She'd spent too many years traveling economy class, knees pressed against the back of the seat in front, not to enjoy the comfort of this luxury flight.

Although she'd been told they'd only be in the air a few hours, she'd found herself undressed within seconds of entering the bedroom. And it had come as a relief to resume their physical intimacy after the tensions of the wedding. The marriage ceremony had had little to do with the connection between them, which neither could deny. But here, there was only the two of them and she could forget everything except the sensation of Harrison inside of her, of his breath against her warm skin, and of his lips opening over hers, connecting with her at a level that needed no words.

When the captain announced they'd be landing in half an hour, Harrison emerged from the shower and came and sat on the side of the bed. He trailed a fingernail over her breasts. "I think you'd better get ready to land. Otherwise, I'll have to carry you naked across the tarmac to Immigration."

She pulled a face at him. "I think I'm a bit too big for you to carry me anywhere."

She squeaked as he slid his hands under her and picked her up effortlessly. He kissed her. "I like how you don't seem worried about the naked part, only the part about me carrying you." She grinned and kissed him back. "Because I know there is no way that my macho man would want any man looking at his wife naked. Am I right, or am I right?" she teased.

He scowled. "You're right, of course." He strode over to the bathroom door. "Now, I haven't carried you over any threshold yet, so here we are." He stepped into the luxurious bathroom.

"I'll expect the same when we return to Marsh House."

"I didn't realize you were so demanding."

"Better believe it."

He lowered her to standing, and she linked her hands around his neck, pressing her stomach and breasts against him.

"I can't wait until I get my body back and I'm not lumbering around, needing help with everything."

He cradled her stomach. "And I can't wait for you to get your body back, too," he said with a sexy smile.

"So I see," she said, stroking his erection, knowing that he was being careful with her at the moment and that he wanted her more often than he was prepared to take her.

He growled. "You're teasing me, woman. Any more of that and I'll take you back to bed."

"No, you won't, because as you said, we will soon be landing." Laughing, she stepped away and turned on the shower. "Aren't you going to tell me where we're going yet?"

"No. Not yet."

"I wonder why," she said with a smile. "Although I

guess it's somewhere in Europe, if we're going to be landing soon."

"You'll see soon enough," he said, leaving the bathroom to get dressed.

She stepped under the shower.

And this, she thought, was the second best thing money could buy. A hot shower, after an afternoon in bed with the man she loved. She grinned and lifted her head up to the shower head, allowing her need to ease under the stream of cool water and to focus herself on the honeymoon ahead. She wondered where it would be. So long as it wasn't freezing, she didn't mind.

BUT THE MOMENT she stepped off the plane, she changed her mind. She knew the country even before she heard anyone speak the native language. She knew the light, she knew the architecture of the buildings as they swept into the airport. And above all, she knew the airport. She didn't need to see the signs to understand where Harrison had brought her. Or why.

"Naples, Harrison, really? Of all the places in the world you knew I didn't want to come, it was to Italy."

"As I said, it's the one place I knew you had to come. You can't run forever, Paris. We can't continue to keep a low profile because of your past. You have to face it some-time. And it may as well be now."

All the pleasures of the afternoon were swept away by his words. Harrison hadn't changed. He still intended to control her, and that spelled trouble on many counts. Including one big one. Harrison didn't know what the hell he was letting him, and her, in for.

CHAPTER 18

*E*verything about Paris revealed her anger. From her foot which swung back and forward from her crossed legs, to her hands gripped together as if scared one of them would strike him if loosed, not to mention the glare she shot at him from time to time. Despite the dark looks, he preferred her glares to the stony stare out the limo window to the Italian countryside. At least it was some connection. But her anger didn't faze him. He was certain that they couldn't continue as they had been. It was time for her to face up to her past.

He hooked one leg over his other knee and sat back. "It couldn't be postponed any longer. You know that."

Her eyes flared with anger. "I don't know any such thing! I told you who my father is and yet you still made arrangements, as if what I think counts for nothing!"

"That's not true. I merely think..." He tried to figure out the best way of using the tools with which he was little acquainted—words. He cleared this throat. "I merely think that the sooner we face up to him, the sooner all this nonsense will stop and we can get on with our lives."

"This nonsense, as you call it, will only escalate." Tears glittered in her eyes, and for the first time, a qualm of something like uncertainty flickered through him. "You have no idea who you're dealing with when it comes to my father!"

"All he wants is to have a relationship with you. Let's get this over with and then we can go back to Norfolk."

"And is this how you're going to deal with things in future? Hey? Any time we disagree, you're going to simply ignore what I think, what I feel, and do what you want, anyway. Is that how our life is going to work out?"

It didn't sound like a bad idea to him, but he knew better than to voice this opinion. "No, of course not. But you have to admit that *not* meeting your father was proving more problematic than meeting him. You have to face facts, Paris, he's not going away. When I saw him, I received the strong impression that he's ready for a new relationship with you."

"I don't want any kind of relationship with him and his criminal family. I don't want him to shower us with money gained from God-knows what crimes." She shook her head. "I don't want a bar of that, Harrison."

"Nor me. Trust me, Paris, all I want is for you not to live in hiding from your father, to make peace with him. If he wants anything more, we're out of there. Do you trust me?"

"It's the only reason I got in this car," she whispered, her gaze fixed on the approaching hill, on top of which was her old family home. "You don't know what you've got us in to."

Harrison followed her gaze to the large estate which grew ever larger. She was wrong. He knew exactly what he was walking in to. He wouldn't be walking in to it otherwise.

THE LARGE GATES swung open for them as they approached the outer perimeter of the estate and they drove past some stone buildings set amidst an olive grove. Despite their rustic appearance, Paris knew these buildings housed state-of-the-art security systems and her father's 'staff'. She had learned from her mother that, in reality, her father's 'staff' were thugs capable of anything, there to protect him, those closest to him, those of value to him. She just hoped that once they were inside, they'd be able to leave.

After they'd gone through the second sets of gates, they entered a different world. A large stretch of emerald-green lawn enclosed a marble fountain, a replica of the Fountain of the Naiads in Rome, a fountain infamous for its naked water nymphs which were reputed to have been modeled on prostitutes. Paris had no reason to not believe the same had happened here. Despite being married, her father had never kept his mistresses a secret.

Paris looked through the car window at the sprawling ancient palazzo. It was as beautiful as she remembered when she'd turned and taken one last look that night so long ago when she'd run away.

The car doors banged and echoed around the seemingly empty palazzo. But she knew there would be people there. There always were. Suddenly her skin prickled, and she looked up in time to see a movement away from the central balcony of the first floor living room. Her father had watched her arrive. She knew it.

"The sooner we get inside and meet him, the sooner we can get the hell out of here," Harrison said quietly, obviously affected by the sinister atmosphere of the place. He put his arm protectively around her and they walked up to the front door.

Before they could reach it, the door opened wide, and a woman stood there, super sexy, dark tumbling hair and a big smile on her face.

"*Caio*, Paris!" she called out, walking swiftly towards Paris and embracing her, air kissing her on both cheeks before standing back and looking at her intently. "*Sembri tuo padre*," she said. Paris blanched. She really didn't want to know that she looked like her father.

She smiled politely, wondering who on earth this woman was who welcomed them into her old home, her father's house, headquarters of a mafia family which spanned several continents. "Is my father home?" she asked in English.

"Ah," said the woman, "of course, Luis told me your mother raised you to speak English as your first language, rather than Italian. We'll speak in English, then." She shifted her gaze to Harrison.

"And you must be Signore Richmond."

"Harrison, please," he said, accepting her hand and shaking it politely.

Her eyes flashed with flirtation and she held on to his hand for a little longer than was polite. She leaned in with a raised eyebrow and a smile on her full lips. "Harrison, it is then," she said.

"You have the advantage of me," he said.

She beamed. "I'm Marguerite, Luis's wife."

Paris was glad Marguerite was too busy admiring Harrison to notice her astonished expression. She hadn't even known her father had re-married. But then why should she?

She turned to Paris. "Come in, come in. Luis is just coming down."

They followed Marguerite into the formal sitting room, with its grandiose proportions, frescoes and irreplaceable objets d'art.

"*Mio caro!*" exclaimed Marguerite, as she walked briskly toward an unseen person, her high heels tapping sharply on the marble floor. "*Guarda chi è qui per vederti!*"

Paris suspected her father knew who was here to see him. After all, her own husband had arranged it with him. When Marguerite moved out of the way to reveal her father, Paris's heart sank. He hadn't changed in the slightest. He stood, tall, slim and elegant, his thick white hair slicked back, accentuating his sharp cheekbones and sensuous mouth. But there *was* one major difference—he stood alone. Usually, he never went anywhere—not even his own home—without being accompanied by two thickset guards. Before she knew any better, she'd believed them to be his friends.

"Papa!" she greeted him, walking forward, and he did something unexpected. He opened his arms, and instinct drew her into them. She kissed his cheeks. His arms closed gently around her and suddenly she was a child again, believing her father loved her best of everyone in the world, and that he was a good man, a noble man, a man worthy of her love. Without thinking, she rested her head against his chest and listened to the steady beat of his heart, remembering a time so long ago when she'd used to do exactly this. But that was before she knew what he did to make his millions, and had been sickened by it.

She pulled away, confused by the maelstrom of emotions which surged through her. He held onto her shoulders. Then she noticed his eyes—tears glistened in them.

"Let me look at you, *cara*." He sighed and shook his head. "Even more beautiful than I remember." He looked across the room at the woman. "Did I not tell you, Marguerite?"

"You did, my darling, and you were right. Even more beautiful pregnant."

"It's been too long, Paris. Far too long. I thought I'd never see you again. You disappeared into the night without a word."

"You'd left me no choice, Papa."

"Come," said Marguerite brightly, obviously not wanting the meeting to sour so quickly. "I've arranged drinks to be brought to us on the patio."

They followed Luis and Marguerite outside onto the terrace. Paris looked around in surprise, expecting to see the usual hangers-on. There had always been a small, tight group hanging around her father to see to his every need, whether that be keeping people away from him or amusing him. But now, they appeared to be alone.

"Where is everyone?" she asked, sitting on the chair on which Marguerite had thoughtfully placed extra cushions.

Her father gestured with his hands. "There is no one anymore. Not since I passed control of the company to Adolfo."

Paris overlooked the euphemism of the word 'company', astounded by what her father had said. "Cousin Adolfo?"

Luis inclined his head in agreement. "Indeed."

"So you're no longer head of the *company*?"

"No." He smiled sadly. "*Cara*," he said, petting her hand. "Relax and have a drink. You must be tired after your travels."

It didn't seem like her father was going to be hurried into telling her what on earth had happened to make him cede control to someone else.

Harrison and Marguerite made small talk while the maid brought them drinks and antipasti. It was only when they were alone that her father gave her a sad smile.

"You have no idea how long I have been imagining this moment."

"He has, you know," said Marguerite.

"But I understand, *cara*," he continued, "what you discovered that night, it was too much for you. And with your mother gone, you no longer felt you had to stay to act as a go-between. I understand."

She was astounded. "You sound like you've had therapy."

Both Luis and Marguerite threw their heads back and laughed. "Indeed," he said. He looked at her over the top of his sunglasses. "I am thoroughly therapized. Thanks to Marguerite. She was the therapist. And I have to say she's gone above and beyond to bring me back from a very dark place."

They exchanged a loving look, before Marguerite turned to Paris with a satisfied smile. "And you're the final link. Now everything will be all right."

Paris tried to smile, but could hardly agree. He may have changed outwardly, but he was the same man who'd run a criminal gang for decades and who had earned a reputation for showing no mercy.

She opened her mouth to dispute Marguerite's statement, but Harrison gave her hand a squeeze and spoke before she could.

"And we both want it to be all right, too. But I think that might take a little more time to work through. Let's just take it a step at a time."

Paris's mouth opened in surprise as she stared at him. Harrison shrugged, as if he didn't know where his words of diplomacy had come from. For someone who professed to be useless with words, he seemed to have just defused a difficult moment.

"Your husband is a wise man, *cara*. Marguerite is being optimistic as usual. But I have hopes now too, hopes I never had before. We have a future now and we will do as you say, Harrison. Slowly, step by step, yes?"

"Yes," she said. She could agree to that. Step by step. Isn't that what you had to do to move on in life? One step at a time until you found you'd emerged and found a different world around you. She'd always been scared that that world ahead of her would be filled with more fear, more treachery. But for the first time in her life, she thought things might be different. Her eyes filled with tears at all the missed opportunities, missed moments they could have had if he'd changed sooner.

"Now," said Marguerite. "Tell me when the baby is due."

But Paris was incapable of saying anything. Harrison helped out.

"In a few weeks. That's why we came straight away."

"And is it going to be a boy or a girl?"

"It's going to be a boy." He looked at Paris. "And he's going to be called Luca."

Paris blinked and jumped up, and walked inside as the tears began to roll in earnest. It was the first time that Harrison had agreed with her on the name, and it represented so much more. His acceptance of her wishes showed his feelings were there, whether or not he denied them. She didn't need words, she told herself. She only needed to know that he cared for her. And she knew that now, deep in her bones now, without being told.

"Are you all right?" She looked around to find Harrison had followed her inside. "What's the matter?"

She shook her head and swept her hair off her face, swiping the tears away and sniffing. "It's all such a shock. From being so alone." She swept open her arms. "To all of this." She cupped her stomach. "Only a few months ago, I thought I'd have to do this all on my own."

"And that was my and your father's fault. But you don't have to do it on your own anymore."

"I know. And that's what's so shocking to me. I can hardly believe it."

"Come on, let's go back to your father and Marguerite. You've got a lot of catching up to do before we leave."

She smiled and, hand in hand, they went back outside into the shady loggia to build relationships.

IN THE END, they stayed two nights in Italy. They couldn't risk any longer because of the baby's due date, but had left with promises of return with Luis's grandson later in the year. Despite her happiness at the reunion, Paris was relieved to be back on the plane. The aches and pains of her body were changing and she knew that Luca wouldn't be long in arriving.

Harrison took her bag from her and put it to one side. "Now, woman, I want you on the bed," he said, with mock sternness.

She laughed. "Why? Do you want to see a heavily pregnant woman sleep?"

He kissed her. "I didn't know you were a mind-reader as well as all the other things you excel at."

She lay on the bed and immediately relaxed. She felt physically and emotionally exhausted. She closed her eyes for a moment and inhaled a deep, calming breath. When she opened them again, she saw he was frowning.

"I don't seem to be much good at reading minds at the moment," Paris said. "What's causing that frown?"

"I'm worried we shouldn't have come. You look exhausted."

"I am. Part of me is glad that I'm no longer running from him. That was a constant nightmare. But another part is wondering what the hell I've just done. He might no longer be head of the firm and he may have fallen in love at long last, but he's the same man who was the head of the family firm for decades. He did things... such things, Harrison, that I hope I never have to describe to you." She blinked, trying to hold back the tears at the invasion of unwanted memories.

"I can imagine what they are. But they are *his* crimes, which *he* will have to make peace with. You had nothing to do with them."

"But how can I be on friendly terms with a man capable of such violence?"

"Because he's your father. He's a complex man, just like my own father, just like all of us."

"But is reconciling with him forgiving him? And, if it is, should I have?"

He shrugged. "I don't know. I'm no moral philosopher. All I know is that it feels right."

"Yes, it certainly feels right to do it."

"He says he's changed, Marguerite says he's changed, and he certainly appears to have changed. So I'd give him the benefit of the doubt and accept him for who he is now. He said he regrets the things he's done, so we can only take him at his word."

"I guess so." She huffed out a relieved sigh and felt the tension drain out of her. "I don't think I realized how much anger I was holding inside until now." She smiled at him and reached out and touched his lips. "It's so much better now that's gone."

"Why? What's replaced it?" he asked, kissing her finger.

"Love. For you, for Luca, and maybe, just maybe, for my father and Marguerite. You know, I don't think I could ever again live without love in my life."

Harrison's smile faltered, and he glanced at the clock and stepped away. "You should get some sleep. We'll be landing soon."

He switched off the light and left the room so abruptly that for a moment Paris wondered if everything was all right with him. And then sleep overcame her, and she drifted into a deep and dreamless sleep.

CHAPTER 19

*E*ven the sun seemed to shine more brightly, thought Paris, as Harrison drove the car slowly along the steep, narrow Blakeney lanes, down to the quay. It was mid-day in the normally sleepy village. A group of teenagers jumped off the bus, laughingly shouting insults at each other, while a young mother pushed a stroller up the steep street and an elderly couple greeted her. Christmas lights were strung along the street and the Salvation Army played carols on the waterfront. Passersby gathered around them, blocking the road.

Paris remembered the last Christmas she'd spent at home in Italy and shuddered. She didn't want to remember that unhappy time. She had now, and now was looking pretty great.

She glanced at Harrison, who, aside from a light tapping on the wheel, didn't betray any impatience. She smiled to herself and looked straight ahead to the glistening water of the quay, which lay at the end of the street. He was a patient man, and he also had compassion.

Which, whether or not he wanted to, betrayed the fact that he had a big heart. Trouble was, he didn't know it. But he would. She'd make sure of it.

When eventually they drove up to the house, she laughed as she peered at its front.

"Marie has been busy."

The bay-fronted windows had Christmas lights around them, and there also appeared to be a heavily decorated tree.

Harrison followed her gaze. "Marie asked if she could decorate while we were away. I gave her permission. I hope you don't mind."

"No. It looks lovely and festive." She heaved a happy sigh. "It's not something I could have contemplated a few weeks ago. But now..." She smiled at him as she brought their joined hands to her lips and kissed the back of his hand.

He raised an eyebrow. "Now?" he prompted.

"Now it seems perfect."

She couldn't understand the sudden frown on his face as he looked away.

"You can't expect perfection, Paris," he said quietly. "Not from me, anyway. Because I'm not and never will be."

"I don't expect anything. I've spent too long with zero expectations to change now. No," she said, looking back at the house. "It's more that I can see a way forward, which isn't turbulent and full of mistrust. We'll have our baby, and there won't be any more shadows over us. There will just be us making a life for ourselves. And that, believe me, sounds very good. Perfect, in fact."

Harrison was saved from answering by the front door

swinging wide and Marie emerging with a big welcoming smile.

"Are you ready?" he asked Paris.

"For what?"

"This," he said, picking her up with one sweeping move and carrying her over the threshold.

THE NEXT DAY, Harrison wondered why he'd suggested going Christmas shopping in the nearby Georgian market town of Holt. It was crowded compared to the windswept quayside village of Blakeney, and he'd always hated crowds. But when Paris emerged from a shop, with bags hanging off her arms and a smile whose brilliance outshone the lights, he knew why. He'd do anything to make her happy.

"What a great place! I've bought things for everyone."

"It looks like it. I'm surprised the store has anything left," he said with a smile.

"I've got a cashmere wrap for Indra and a beautiful pewter platter for Lily's new home. She told me she'd been looking for one exactly like it."

"I'm sure they'll love them," he said, not having a clue whether or not they would. But he certainly loved how happy Paris looked.

She pulled out her phone. "I need to text Indra. I've forgotten who she said Sebastian's favorite designer was." She frowned at her phone. "Darn, it's dead. Remind me to charge it in the car."

"Sure."

"It's wonderful to feel free, you know? Not have to hide anymore."

"Thank God we got it sorted."

"I can hardly believe it myself. Thank goodness for Marguerite. She's certainly changed him." She frowned suddenly. "Do you think he's really changed? For good?"

He shrugged. "We can but hope. He certainly seems okay with allowing you to lead your own life now, and that's all that matters. Anything else is icing on the cake." He wanted that smile back on her face and so opened one of her bags. "So, what else did you buy in the store?" One glance had told him the kind of things they stocked. It had been full of soft, muted colors, and beautiful textures. "Nothing for me, Alex or Seb, I hope."

She laughed. "No, but I've got this for Luca." She opened a bag, and he saw a doll inside.

"A doll, Paris? Really?"

"It's cute."

"Dolls are for girls. If you give that to him, he'll grow up too soft."

She stopped walking suddenly. Was it something he said? She frowned and then rubbed her back.

"Fancy a coffee?"

She sagged, revealing her tiredness. "That would be lovely."

They stepped inside a café, and after finding a table by the window for Paris, he ordered two coffees and enough food for the three of them.

He returned to the table to find her looking wistfully out. The lights cast a glow on her cheekbones and lips, highlighting her beauty. But then she shifted her gaze slightly, and he saw she looked a little sad, although she always presented a smile when she was with him. He remembered the previous night when she'd told him she loved him and he knew it wasn't a statement so much as a question. A question he hadn't answered.

His thoughts were interrupted by the waitress bringing over the coffees. After she'd left, he noticed Paris was laughing at him.

"What have I done?" He didn't actually care what he'd done. In fact, he'd do it again just to see her laugh.

"Do you know how incongruous you look in a small-town café?"

He loved that grin and returned it. "If it's anything like how uncomfortable I feel, then I do."

She reached over and took his hand. "We don't have to stay here, you know, not if you don't want to. We can go anywhere now."

"Do you really want to live in the world I once inhabited? Constant travel, lots of small talk, parties, meeting the same people at each polo event, drinking the same drinks. You know the kind of thing."

"I don't, thank goodness, but I can imagine. But, put like that, and it doesn't sound appealing."

"It's not. Not to me anymore, anyway. I've cut my ties with the polo scene."

"What are you going to do?"

"Look after you, for one thing."

"Harrison!"

"I know. You don't need looking after. Is it okay if I simply say I want to be with you, hang out with you and the baby, make a life together here?"

"That is perfectly okay. Except..." She frowned.

"Except what?"

"You'll be bored. You need something other than me, Luca, and managing your finances."

Her perceptiveness never failed to surprise him. He'd come across so few people in his life who put him first, who were interested in making him happy.

"You're right, of course. I've been talking to Sebastian about their horses and we'll probably work together to build up the equestrian center side of the business."

Her face lit up as if she loved horses, which he knew she didn't. She was terrified of them. "That's perfect! You'll love that and you'll be able to see your brother regularly."

He pulled a pretend face. "I guess there's always a downside to everything."

She laughed, knowing he was joking.

"And I can take Luca over to Richmond Estate and get him involved, too," he said.

Her smile faded. "Of course, if he's interested. You have to be prepared for the fact he might prefer cooking or reading or playing with dolls."

"He's a boy, for goodness' sake!"

"Harrison," she said, placing her coffee cup quietly onto its saucer. "You know, our son will be raised to be who he wants to be. If that's soft, that's fine. If that's, well, a bit tougher, that's fine too. But I'm concerned you want him to be some tough, macho boy. He might not be like that."

He understood what she was saying, but it went against the grain. "He's a boy, Paris. He'll have to be tough in the playground, and later at work. Having him grow up soft won't do him any favors."

"Nor is forcing him to be someone he isn't." She reached over and took his hand. How could he resist the warmth in her eyes? "Please, just think about it. I know it's different to how you were raised, but that didn't do *you* any favors, did it?"

He frowned, hating that she was right.

"Please?" she asked.

He grunted assent. "How about I allow him to play with dolls if you allow him to come hunting with me?"

"Hunting?" she said, surprised.

"Yes, hunting."

"What kind of hunting?"

"Hunting wild animals. Deer, boars, you know."

"No way! I don't want him hunting."

"And I don't want him wrapped in cotton wool, playing with dolls."

She sucked in a deep breath, and he could sense a compromise coming. "We haven't even had Luca yet. How about we figure it out as we go?"

He nodded. But there was no way any son of his was going to be wearing a dress, or sitting around being inactive. No way at all.

ALL THE WAY HOME, their conversation re-played in Paris's mind. Her relationship with Harrison had grown exponentially for the better over a brief period. But she was concerned at his refusal to contemplate anything 'soft', anything to do with affection or, God forbid, anything that required him to say the word 'love'.

That he hadn't told her he loved her hurt more than she cared to reveal to him. She knew he had it in him, but also knew his pride refused to allow him to acknowledge it. She could just about cope with him not acknowledging his love for her. But Luca? She certainly couldn't cope with the thought that he might not show his love for their child.

As unwilling as she was to disturb their newly found peace and happiness right before Christmas, she knew she had to talk with him about it. Maybe after Christmas. Maybe then. But, as she felt a pain in her back, reminding her that Luca would emerge soon, she knew it couldn't wait.

CHAPTER 20

That evening, Harrison looked across the marshes at the fire that briefly swept over the mud flats and grasses before being swallowed by the horizon. He wondered what felt different. And then he realized. He felt at peace. It was strange to feel grounded, with no urge to grab a bag and jump on the nearest plane to the next thing which would amuse him.

As darkness descended over the flat land, with the sand dunes catching a last lick of gold, the sea was blood red, and he wished, above all things, that he could love, like Paris loved. But he couldn't. He never came over emotional, he never could shift the leaden lump in his chest, never make it leap or do anything. He had to face it. He could give Paris anything except love.

He watched as she wrapped presents and laid them under the tree. Christmas Day was still a week away, but Paris seemed to be intent on enjoying all the traditions. He smiled to himself as he imagined the Christmases which lay ahead of them. Then she looked up and his smile disappeared. There were shadows under her eyes and she moved awkwardly, as if in pain. He flexed his hands, to try to control the tingling he felt there when he sensed her discomfort and was worried at the pain she would experience giving birth. He could and would do anything for her, he knew—anything but love her.

She looked up and smiled. "You look far away."

"No, I was here, with you, thinking about you."

She smiled and raised an eyebrow. "Only nice things, I hope?"

"Paris, there is no way I would think not nice things about you."

"Good. So come here and give me a kiss."

He did as she suggested but couldn't completely banish the sense of lack on his part.

She looked up at him with a frown. "What's wrong?"

"I guess I'm just concerned that I will never give you what it is you want."

"How do you know what I want?"

He grunted in amusement. "You told me. Quite clearly once. You said you wanted to be loved."

"Ah, yes. I remember. And that's worrying you?"

He took his time before answering, brushing a strand of her hair back from her face, and laying it against the others. By the time he looked back into her eyes, concern was etched in them. She was still waiting for an answer.

He nodded.

"Harrison, our lives have changed so much in the last few months that I'm sure they will keep on changing."

"I'm a cold man, Paris. You should know that by now."

She shook her head. "I don't believe it."

His heart felt even colder. "That's what I'm afraid of."

The door banged open, and Marie brought in some baking fresh from the oven and hot drinks before she left for the night.

As the evening progressed, so did the sense of despair that he wasn't enough for Paris. She was happy for now because of how much their relationship had developed. And, no doubt, she believed it would continue to develop. But later, when she realized he was right, and he had no love in him for anyone, would she be happy then? He knew the answer. His Paris would never be happy without the love she needed and craved and deserved.

He managed to hide his thoughts from her throughout the evening but, when, much later, they were in bed, she moved in his arms and lifted that beautiful face to him in query.

"You're still fretting, aren't you?" she asked.

He kissed the top of her head and tightened his arms around her. She snuggled into his body.

"I guess."

"Why?" She tried to move around in his arms to face him but he held her more tightly, distracting her with a kiss on the neck and a caress of her breasts, which he hoped would stop the questions. "Why?" she repeated. His heart sank.

"Because one day you'll discover that what I say is true. I'm damaged goods, Paris. There's no way I can reclaim my heart. No way I can love."

She lay still for a few moments. "What do you think you are doing now?"

"Holding you, caring for you and Luca."

"And don't you think caring is close to love? No, more than that, caring is an expression of love."

He released her and rolled back onto the bed. "Paris! Don't you see? You're hoping for something which isn't there, will *never* be there. And that scares me."

She rolled onto her side, propped herself up on her elbow and placed her hand on his chest, searching his face. He wished his eyes weren't watering. He blinked, unsure why they were.

"Why does my belief that you can love scare you?"

"Because 'belief' and 'hope' aren't solid things on which to base a marriage. One day you'll wake up, realize I was right, and you'll walk out that door."

"And what do you consider *are* solid things on which to base a marriage?"

"The reasons we married in the first place. To create a secure home for our son, to make sure he feels wanted."

"And that's enough for you?"

"It has to be. Isn't that enough for you?" he asked.

"No." She pulled her hand from his chest and sat up. He immediately put his own hand where hers had been. She looked away, her hair tumbled all around her, hiding her expression.

"Paris?"

When she did turn to him her gaze was fierce, and tears tracked down her cheeks.

"No, I married you because I loved you. We married for better or for worse, we married in sickness and in health, we married to be together for the rest of our lives. *That's* why I married you! I'd never marry anyone simply for expedience. You're right," she said angrily. "We *are* different."

"I *know* we are. And that's what concerns me. I can't give you what you want, Paris. I just can't. It's not in me."

He tried to reach out for her, needing her touch, but she batted away his hands and stood up, pulling on her robe. "Then perhaps you should leave." There was a cold finality to the statement which chilled him.

"It's been preying on my mind," he said.

She turned blazing eyes on to him. "You're thinking of leaving me? All the time we've been preparing for Christmas, me, talking about how happy I am, and you've been thinking of leaving me?"

"It's not like it sounds."

"How can it be anything different to how it sounds? Are you thinking of leaving me?"

"My reasons for being with you still stand. Luca."

"That's not enough for me."

"I know, and I don't think it's enough for me any longer—" He didn't get a chance to explain further, to untangle his thoughts before she exploded.

"Then why bother waiting around? Why not leave now? This instant! What are you waiting for?"

"You need me, and—"

"For the last time! I do *not* need you!"

"You're about to give birth to our child. I can't leave you now."

"Harrison, if you don't love me and are planning to leave me, believe me, I don't want you to wait. I don't want to be waking up every morning and looking to see if you're there or not. I'd rather you leave now and be done with it."

He lay silent for a few moments. He'd known it would come to this, just hadn't expected it would come so soon. He knew that, for once in his life, he had no choice in this. He'd do anything for her now, even leave.

"I'll do whatever you want me to do."

"I want you to go."

It was like an ice-cold shaft of pain sliced through his body. He felt sick to his stomach. He swallowed dryly. "I'll go in the morning."

"No! Once before, I asked you to leave, and you didn't. You refused. I'm asking you again to go. Go now. I don't want you here. Understand?"

He understood alright. A few months ago, he'd have refused to leave. He would have demanded that they be together because of his need to do the right thing by his son. To not have history repeat itself. But now? Everything had changed. He no more wanted to force Paris to his will than fly. He didn't examine the urge, simply acted on it.

He swung his legs off the bed and held his head briefly in his hands before jumping up and walking out the connecting door to his bedroom. As he dressed, he listened for her footsteps, hoping she'd come to tell him she'd changed her mind. Because he realized he *had* to leave unless she told him he could stay. He was completely at her mercy. Whatever she wanted him to do, he'd do. He owed her that much.

But there had been nothing but silence from her as he threw some things into a bag, looked around the room briefly, marveling at how different he felt now to how he'd felt when he'd first moved in here with Paris. It seemed like years ago, not months. He paused in the hallway and closed his eyes against his tears, listening for any sound from Paris, any sign that she'd changed her mind. There was none. Only the wind battering the house and the sound of rain clattering against the window. What he'd imagined had come to pass, but he'd never imagined he'd feel so bad. He continued outside, the wind nearly whipping the door from his grasp as he descended the steps and battled the wind and rain along the sea-lashed causeway to the car.

Where would he go? His instinct was to do exactly as she said and disappear from her life to show her he meant it. Once, only months earlier, he'd wanted to capture her, hold her close and never let her go. Now, he simply wanted to free her. She was more important to him now than he was. He had no choice but to do what she asked of him and to leave. With a heavy heart, he started up the car and drove away.

PARIS DIDN'T KNOW how long she'd sat—shell-shocked and grief-stricken—after she'd heard his car drive off. A part of her hadn't believed he would actually leave. But he had. A few months ago, he'd forced his way into her life, making sure she couldn't leave. But now? Now, he'd gone because he said he wanted her to have her freedom from a man who could never love her. Only a man in love would do that. Shame he didn't realize it. But he would.

But not tonight, it seemed. She sat with her head in her hands, trying to ward off the throbbing headache which was a consequence of her tears. In the end, she rose and automatically went to the kitchen to get a hot drink. She kept her hand resting on the kettle as she looked out at the black night in which the storm raged, invisibly. She felt strangely aloof, as if she were at sea, alone, but safely cocooned. He'd come back. She knew he would.

Suddenly the lights snapped off, and the kettle ceased bubbling beneath her hand. The room was pitched into blackness, unrelieved from the streetlights at the end of the causeway. She groped her way from window to window, checking the coastline and houses for signs of electricity, but all was in darkness. The storm must have damaged a central power line somewhere.

Candles. Matches. She hadn't stocked this house and didn't know whether there were, in fact, any of the things she'd need, like a torch. She tried a few drawers with no success. Then she remembered where her handbag was and withdrew her phone. It sprung into life before immediately dying. She closed her eyes and pressed the phone against her forehead with dread. She'd forgotten to charge it in the car. She tried the house phone. It was dead and she could hear why. The phone wire banged against the side of the house. She was cut off. She'd never felt so alone before and was appalled at how easily it had happened.

Swallowing down the fear and refusing to allow her imagination full rein, she returned to bed. She'd sleep this awful night away. That's what she'd do. She lay there trying to meditate, trying to calm her racing heart. But her body refused to co-operate. She needed to visit the bathroom, and it was only when there was a rush of fluid before she could reach the toilet that she realized what had happened. Her waters had broken. The pressure she'd been experiencing inside of her all day deepened and sharpened into a sudden debilitating pain which had her crying out loud and falling onto her knees, slumped over the side of the bath.

When at last the wave of intense pain passed, she rolled back onto her haunches and looked up at the bathroom ceiling, her eyes awash with tears. Her baby was coming, and she was all alone with no means of communicating with anyone. What the hell was she going to do?

etween labor pains, which were coming thick and fast now, Paris pulled on her coat and walked carefully down the stairs to the hallway. She braced herself before flinging the front door open wide. Rain lashed at her, and she was soaked within seconds. But, bent double, she forced herself to step outside into the gusty wind, holding on to the iron railing for dear life. With the heel of her hand, she pushed away her hair, searching the Blakeney quayside for any signs of life. But it was late now. The pubs had closed and, it being in the middle of winter and a gale, there was no sign of anyone either in the street or in their homes. But they'd be there. Someone *had* to be there.

With her head down, she thrust first one foot then another along the causeway. Then she had another contraction, and she had no choice but to drop to the ground on all fours on the muddy path and breathe her way out of it. She let out a wail of frustration and fear as the contraction gripped her. By the time it had passed, she felt weak and chilled. When she looked up, she thought she was hallucinating. A bright light was shining straight at her. She squinted and one light became two, and she suddenly realized she was looking directly into the head-lights of a car. She hadn't heard it approach over the whine of the wind.

A door slammed, and she tried to get up, but her limbs refused to cooperate. She struggled again and heard a shout, but couldn't tell who had shouted or what they'd said as the sound fractured in the wind. Suddenly, powerful arms slid under her and lifted her up.

"Paris!" said a voice she hardly recognized, such was the surprise and fear in it.

She looked up through the rain to the shadowy figure. She couldn't believe what she was seeing. "I thought you'd gone."

"Christ, Paris! Are you all right?" He pushed away the hair which was plastered to her cheeks. "What the hell are you doing?"

She was so relieved to see him she felt suddenly weak, and he had to hold her more firmly. "Doing?" She gave a grim laugh. "Having a baby, of course. Why the hell do you think I'd be out in weather like this?"

"The baby? He's coming now?" He swore and looked around, gripping her more firmly. "Let's get you in the car."

They managed to walk along the causeway without slipping. Harrison held her tightly, as if his life depended on it. Her life did, as did the life of their child, that much was certain. He flung open the car door.

Rain splattered onto the leather seats, darkening them in moments, as he lowered her onto the back seat. But

Paris was too soaked to be aware of anything other than the need to lie curled up on her side, and focus on her breathing.

"I'll get something to keep you warm," he said, popping the boot.

She eased herself into a more comfortable position as Harrison re-appeared and gently tucked a blanket around her. He leaned in and kissed her.

"Don't worry about a thing. You'll be fine. I'll make sure of it."

"Where did you go?"

"Not far. I couldn't leave you. I just couldn't. So I turned around and came straight back." He kissed her again.

She fell back against the seat while he jumped into the driver's seat, turned the heat on high and drove carefully over the rutted drive to the road, talking all the while, words which he normally never used, words to comfort and reassure her.

The journey to the hospital seemed to take twice as long as it normally did. Each mile contained tears, cries and labored breathing as Paris tried to keep calm and manage the pain. And each mile contained moments of utter peace—her cheek pressed against the leather seat of the car, as she cradled her stomach with one hand and listened to Harrison. His words flowed like they'd never done before. She'd known this man of few words would find them when he needed them. And it seemed he needed them now. And so did she.

He was so strong. From her vantage point, she could see his hands firmly gripping the steering wheel and his gaze fixed on the road, occasionally glancing at her in the rearview mirror. Even then, the frown was one of strength and determination, and she knew she was in the very best of hands. She knew, with absolute certainty, that he would get her safely to the hospital. After all, as a polo player, he was known for his nerve of iron and a cold heart. *El hombre de corazón frío*, they called him—the cold-hearted man. And she was thankful for it now, even while she knew it wasn't all of him. There was much more beneath that facade which he had yet to discover.

"We're close now."

But she didn't hear because she'd raised herself onto all fours and was panting as the pressure increased and the pain grew unbearable. Dimly she was aware of the car drawing to a halt, of the car door whipping open and eyes peering in at her. She blinked at the light.

"Lie back there a moment," said a reassuring voice, "and let us check you out quickly. I'm Pam," said the motherly voice, as she moved aside Paris's clothes to do a quick assessment. "Perfect," she said with a broad smile. "Your little one will arrive shortly, so let's get you inside out of this weather, shall we?"

Without waiting for an answer, the woman's face disappeared and Harrison leaned in, swept his hands under her and pulled her out of the car. She'd never been so relieved in her life to have a journey end. She leaned against his chest with a sob as he ignored everyone else and strode into the warmth and shelter of the hospital. She was vaguely aware of people running around, and then Harrison laying her gently on a trolley bed.

She felt bereft when he stepped away—despite all the professional people around her, she wanted only one person with her.

"Harrison!" she cried out. "Don't leave me!"

"I won't," he said firmly, taking her hand and walking beside her as they pushed the trolley further into the hospital, through banging doors. She was given some gas and air and she lay on her back watching the overhead lights flow past her. Between the rhythmic rattle of the wheels, the midwife's chat about everyday things, and the firm grip of Harrison's hand over hers, she began to feel calmer. Until they laid her on the bed and another contraction gripped her. When it passed, she was distantly aware of nurses and the midwife milling around, and Harrison still holding her hand. For one long moment they looked at each other—their eyes expressing the full gamut of emotion—from concern, to hope, to relief to something much more intense, something much more reassuring. And, in that moment, Paris knew she didn't need the words for what she could see in his heart.

The moment passed as pain shot through her body. She'd wanted a natural childbirth and it turned out it was too late for anything else. She felt everything with intensity and, between the midwife's professionalism and Harrison's love, she took control, gathered the last of her strength and pushed for all she was worth. In the end, it only took three more contractions before Luca slipped into the world calmly and with a slightly surprised look on his face. But the surprised look had nothing on Harrison, when the midwife swiftly wrapped Luca and passed him into Harrison's waiting hands.

She didn't think she'd ever forget the look on his face as he held his son for the first time. It was naked. There was no filter between him and the rest of the world, nothing but total awe and love. His eyes filled with tears as he brought Luca to her. She smoothed a finger over Luca's downy head and kissed it.

"Hello, my darling boy," she whispered.

She laughed as he opened his mouth to capture the tip of her finger.

"I think I know what you want, little one," she said, pushing aside her gown. She took him from Harrison and lifted him to her breast. He immediately began suckling.

"You have a very peaceful baby there," said Pam with a smile.

"Goodness knows why, given the circumstances of his birth!" said Paris with a laugh. "We nearly had him in the car!"

"He's calm and focused," Harrison said, with a smile which hadn't left his face since Luca's birth. "Like his mum." His smile broadened as he met her eyes. "There's no shifting them from what they want. And then, suddenly, you don't want to shift them when you realize they were right all along."

Pam looked from one to the other with a smile. "Whichever way you look at it, he's a content boy, and a lucky one to be born into such a loving family." She collected some things and went to the door. "I'll leave you three in peace. If you want anything, ring the bell."

The sounds of the hospital receded after the door closed, leaving only the sound of Luca suckling.

"I can't believe it," said Harrison quietly, leaning forward and pushing the soft blanket back a little so he could see his son's head. "He's so perfect."

Paris shifted her smile from Luca to Harrison. "He is, isn't he?"

"Oh, yes," he said, kissing her cheek. "Nearly as perfect as his mother."

She brushed Luca's soft downy hair gently with the back of her finger. "He's going to be tall, like you," she said, stroking Luca's long legs.

"And with my coloring, by the looks of things. Blue eyes."

She laughed. "All babies are born with blue eyes."

"And he's definitely got your temperament."

"True. He knows what he wants and takes action to get it. Of course, that doesn't always mean you achieve what you want."

"You stand a better chance than *not* taking action," Harrison said, sitting back in his chair. "Like you. Leaving your father's world and creating one for yourself."

She huffed a laugh. "That stopped working the minute you walked into my life."

"You lured me," he said with a kiss. "With your siren song."

"Otherwise known as a Chopin Prelude," she said wryly.

"And then you moved on again, created another new life for yourself."

"Which you, again, disrupted."

"True," he mused, stroking his son's head. "I guess he stood little chance of being docile and passive with parents who both know what they want."

She shot him a look. "Especially when the father won't take no for an answer." She wished she could have taken back the words, because she wanted nothing to come between them. She didn't want to re-hash the past, only move forward. She cleared her throat. "I wonder what you were like as a baby."

Harrison's smile faded. "No idea. Dad never talked about it."

"Sebastian will know. And probably Alexander. Sebastian must have been about eight years old when you were born?"

"Seven."

"I'll ask him next time we see him."

"Ah. About that."

"What?" she said, distracted as she shifted Luca from one breast to the other.

"The next time we see Sebastian."

She looked up and tilted her face in a mock warning query.

"I know you wanted Christmas Day at Blakeney. But when Indra found out—"

"That's fine—"

"She insisted..." He trailed off. "Did you say 'that's fine'?"

"Yep."

"But I thought you were adamant you wanted Christmas at Marsh House."

"I did. But that was then." She shifted the now sleeping Luca in her arms when her nipple popped out of his mouth and adjusted her clothing. "And this is now. Everything is different now."

Harrison suddenly looked uncertain, which was a rarity for him. They still hadn't talked about his disappearance and sudden, timely reappearance. But they would, and then she'd make sure that look of uncertainty disappeared and never came back.

She handed a sleeping Luca to Harrison.

"No!" he said in alarm. "I might drop him."

"Nonsense."

She didn't give him any option. Then she sat back and watched her macho man melt as he held his son, muttering words of endearment which she had no idea he knew, caressing him gently through the soft blanket. And in that moment, she thought she was the happiest woman alive.

CHAPTER 22

As Harrison looked around the drawing room at Richmond Manor, he had to admit that it was the perfect place to celebrate a family Christmas. Since Charlotte's birth, Sebastian and Indra's home had lost some of its formality and had transformed into a family home, with children's toys and other baby paraphernalia dotted around the once formal and pristine room.

Charlotte had begun to cry, so Indra laid her down on a cot beside them. Charlotte enjoyed company and screamed blue murder if she felt she was being put somewhere on her own. She only ever settled with the sound of people and activity around her. Harrison watched as Paris handed Luca to Lily, who had just announced she was four months pregnant. She'd loudly declared she needed practice.

Between the two babies and six adults, not to mention sundry friends and waifs and strays Indra had collected, the place was full of life. Harrison couldn't remember it ever having been that way before. But even as he thought that, memories nudged into his brain, trying to form.

He frowned and looked away from the busyness inside the room, out across the park. Snow had started to fall on the pristine lawns of Richmond Manor, resting lightly on the bare tree branches and frosting the tops of the fountain and stone wall. Minute by minute, the place was metamorphosing into a picture postcard. Transformed from a place that he used to dread visiting—a place which epitomized everything he hated—to one which epitomized everything he'd come to cherish. Family.

At the sound of laughter, he looked around to see Lily had finished telling an anecdote, and Alexander and Sebastian were roaring with laughter. Indra was holding Charlotte, whose little hand had grabbed a fistful of her long dark hair. But she was looking at Harrison. He smiled at her. She'd not only transformed his eldest brother, Sebastian, she'd transformed Richmond Manor. And, in so doing, had transformed all their lives. It was a family home now.

She walked up to him. "You look lost in thought." She followed his gaze out to the sweeping white expanse of the estate which looked bright against the molten dark sky.

"Nothing profound," he said, unwilling to share his innermost thoughts, even with his sister-in-law, of whom he was so fond. "Just remembering when we were very young boys. I guess it must have been before Mother died." He shook his head as if to shrug off the idea. "Anyway, I remember all three of us having a snowball fight out on the lawn. My brothers didn't hold back and, being the youngest, I bore the brunt of it. I seem to remember they tried to pack me with snow like a snowman and fix a carrot on my nose and sunglasses over my eyes."

"And you let them?"

"I didn't have much choice!" He frowned as other dim memories tried to nudge their way into his consciousness. "But then, I seem to remember there was a bang at the window, and Mother shouted to Alex and Seb to stop teasing me." He blinked. "You know, I hadn't remembered that detail before."

"Is there anything else you can remember?" Indra prompted gently. He barely heard her as he re-lived that moment, so long ago. There wasn't anything now to stop him from remembering. No paralyzing fear trying to prevent hurt. Instead, he remembered his mother opening the French doors and striding out to them. It must have been when she was well. Before the illness.

"Alexander! Sebastian! Stay right where you are!" she'd shouted.

Alexander and Sebastian had stopped what they were doing and looked at each other, not wanting to disobey their beloved mother, but not wanting to stop the fun, either. Their mother's face was fierce as she'd stepped towards them. Then, when she was within range, she bobbed down and scooped up handfuls of snow before they realized what she was doing. Snowballs started flying at them with full force. One hit Sebastian directly on the nose.

"Come on, Harry!" she'd called. "Come and give me a hand sorting these two out!" He'd jumped up and down to clear the snow off him and gone running to his mother. And they'd sorted them. He could recall now, with vivid clarity, their laughter creating clouds of vapor and his mother's reddened cheeks and bright eyes. How her curly blonde hair had caught the sunshine, illuminating her in a golden haze. And most of all, he could remember the warmth in her eyes as she looked at him. And how, after the snowball fight, she'd kneeled in the snow before him, wiping away the remaining snow from his hair, and kissed him on the cheek.

"There are two things in this world you mustn't forget, Harry. One, that you need to stand up to those beastly big brothers of yours. And two…"

"Two?" he asked, wondering at her smile.

"Two, I love you so very much, my darling boy. And I always will."

Before anything further could be said, a snowball had landed on the back of his mother's head and disintegrated, showering snow over them both. She laughed, and was soon chasing the boys with more snowballs.

Harrison huffed a disbelieving laugh as the memory faded. *He'd remembered his mother.* He's actually remembered her. In detail. The fine features of her face, how her lips curved into a smile that no one could withstand. What she'd said, what she'd done, and how much they'd loved each other. It felt like a miracle. He turned away from Indra, back to looking outside once more, unwilling to expose himself.

Indra put her hand on his shoulder. "Is everything all right? You look as if you've seen a ghost."

He sucked in a deep breath and looked back to her. "I think I have. But it's a ghost I refused to see before, but now I can. A good memory, Indra. A very good memory."

"Excellent. I hope Richmond Manor will be the source of many more memories to come. For us, and for our children."

She looked at Lily, who was trying to convince Paris that Lily's four-month pregnancy was already showing. It wasn't. They were surrounded by the detritus of opened Christmas presents which mainly comprised children's toys and clothes and indispensable gorgeous things for all three nurseries.

"Especially at Christmas," said Harrison.

"Especially at Christmas," repeated Indra, looking around. "Richmond Manor is a beautiful home but, at Christmas, it really comes into its own."

As Harrison watched Indra return to Sebastian, who had his arms outstretched, ready to receive Charlotte, he couldn't help but think that a lot of the charm of the manor at Christmas was down to Indra. She had spared no expense or trouble and had decorated the manor with tasteful traditional decorations, including at least six real Christmas trees.

He took a minute, reluctant to return to the others. He was still struck by the sudden, vivid memory of his mother. And he knew that memory would be trapped inside if it wasn't for Paris, opening up his heart.

He looked across and saw she was looking at him. She shot him a questioning look. He shook his head and went to join her.

He took Luca from her and cradled him gently in his arms. Paris leaned into him and put her arms around them both.

"Everything okay?"

"More than okay."

And, as his brothers and their wives moved around them, chatting about nothing in particular, making plans for the future and simply being happy in the moment, he knew it was, and it would be, absolutely more than okay. It was the future he was sure his mother had hoped for them all.

"You know I can't imagine you and Luca not being here with me. The lack of you is impossible to comprehend," he said at last.

"You didn't give me much choice, the way you tracked me down and gave me an ultimatum."

Harrison winced. "I never want to be that man again, Paris."

She wriggled closer to him and swept her finger up his chest before resting it on his lips. "You know? That's kind of a shame, because sometimes I quite enjoy that man, and I know, for sure, that he's not gone. He was certainly there last night in bed."

He smiled at the memory. "You know what I mean." He pulled away her hand. "And don't do that, otherwise I'll throw you over my shoulder and take you off to the bedroom and ravish you."

He enjoyed the way her face flushed and her eyes darkened as she imagined what he would do to her.

"As I was saying. I want you to know that I'll never force you to do anything again. You're free to do exactly as you like. You mean too much to me to constrain you."

"Mean too much?" she said, teasing. "What exactly do you mean by that?"

He raised an eyebrow. "You know."

She opened her arms innocently. "How can I know? You haven't told me what I mean to you."

"That was because I didn't know. But I do now."

She gasped, and her eyes opened wide with shock. She

didn't reply. Her complete attention was on what he was about to say.

"I love you. Pure and simple," he said.

"You love me?" she asked, wonderingly. She gave a laugh of disbelief. "You love me?" She wrinkled her brow.

"I love you. I think I always have, but it took a while for me to understand."

She gripped his shoulders. "Tell me again."

"I love you."

She pressed her lips hard against his, as if she needed to feel the words to understand them. She pulled away with a laugh and turned to the others. Indra was holding a sleeping Charlotte. Sebastian and Alexander were talking and Lily sat tapping her stomach as she talked with Indra about pregnancy.

"He loves me!" shouted out Paris.

Everyone looked at her and laughed.

"Of course he does!" said Lily. "Anyone can see that!"

She turned back to Harrison. "Anyone except you, my love. But now you can."

"Now I can," he said softly, before pressing his lips to hers in a kiss which showed that there was now no shadow on his heart, nothing between them except a deep and abiding love, which they both knew would last forever.

"Listen," said Lily, her bright eyes looking toward the front door. Everyone stopped talking and followed her gaze. At first Harrison couldn't hear anything. Then the sound of singing grew louder.

"It'll be the carol singers. They said they'd call by," said Indra. "There are some mince pies warming in the oven.

I'll get them." She passed Charlotte to Sebastian, and they all grabbed their coats and went outside onto the porch.

Dressed in Victorian costumes and carrying a lantern, the small group of villagers and estate workers went through their repertoire of carols, fading out on the high notes before returning to the chorus with gusto. With his arm around Paris and his son sleeping peacefully in the crib in the warm, Harrison looked around his family. He thought about the memory of his mother, knowing there would be more where that came from, and felt a deep contentment such as he'd never felt before.

"This has got to be the best Christmas ever," murmured Paris, her head resting against Harrison's chest.

"The first of many," said Harrison, kissing the top of her head.

THE END

~

Want to read another Diana Fraser romance? Why not try the first book in my Mackenzies series? (Excerpt follows.)

***A Place Called Home**—An art restorer looking for a home. A grief-stricken widower running from his emotions. A painting which brings them together but which reveals a mysterious past from which neither can escape...*

"The storyline was **fantastic & well written**. I was expecting a sweet romance, but it was that & a lot more. It was love. but a twist brings a lot of drama that will keep you on the edge of your seat. Fantastic." (Amazon.com)

"Very good book. Very interesting characters. The story just flows from beginning to end. **You get immersed in the story and can't put it down until you finish**. I highly recommend this author. I will certainly read the other books in this series." (Amazon Canada)

Dear Reader,

This was a bit of a love letter to Norfolk, England, the place I grew up and lived until I was eighteen. I lived in a seaside town just down the road from Blakeney. But Blakeney was our destination for Sunday afternoon walks on the marshes where we'd dig for cockles, slide in the mud and row boats on the river. Writing Harrison and Paris's story brought back many wonderful memories.

I also began learning to play the piano from the age of five and continued until recently. Alas, I'm without a piano at the moment, but hope to remedy that soon. As I wrote the scene where Paris plays the piano, I listened to composers such as Satie and, of course, Chopin.

You can find all my books and discounted book bundles (by far the most cost effective way of reading my books) on my website and store—dianafraser.com. Here, you can also sign up to my email list if you'd like me to drop you a line when my latest release has been published.

Happy reading!

Diana

A PLACE CALLED HOME

BOOK 1 OF THE MACKENZIES—GUY AND LUCIA

An art restorer looking for a home. A grief-stricken widower running from his emotions. A painting which brings them together but which reveals a mysterious past from which neither can escape...

After an itinerant and lonely childhood, art restorer Lucia yearns for what other people have—a home, husband and children. There is no way she's going to get involved with a commit-

ment-phobe again. Guy takes the concept of a commitment-phobe to a whole new level—but with good reason. He's been running from his emotions since his wife's death. But their lives become entwined when Lucia proves his 'forgery' is genuine and reveals a mysterious past from which neither can escape...

Excerpt

Guy switched off the light and seconds turned into minutes as their eyes slowly adjusted to the dark.

He was glad he'd told Lucia about Hannah because there was something about Lucia that attracted him deeply, made him almost forget his intention to remain single. She was independent, compared to Hannah's clinginess, and easygoing, compared to Hannah's hot-headedness. She was also totally gorgeous, inheriting the best of both her Italian and Chinese ancestry—dark and sensual and yet also elegant and slightly aloof, as if wary of this alien world she'd found herself in.

All afternoon he'd taken every opportunity he could to breathe in her scent. To begin with, he'd assumed it was her perfume, but it wasn't artificial enough. Then, as they'd entered the cave and she'd bent her head to adjust her ankle strap, he'd thought it was the shampoo she used. It was only when she stumbled slightly, and he caught her in his arms, and she looked at him, long and slow, that he knew it was simply her. An exquisite mix of everything. And he also knew it was a fragrance he'd never get enough of.

"What—"

"Hush." He squeezed her hand. "Keep quite still and wait."

God help him, all he could do was inhale her. He moved his head slightly toward her and her hair lightly brushed his cheek, sending a shiver of need through his body.

And then it happened.

Slowly the faint lights flickered on. One by one to begin with, then small clusters burst into life. But Guy wasn't looking at them. He knew their ethereal beauty and was more interested in looking at another kind of beauty. His gut tightened as Lucia opened her mouth in a small gasp of wonder. Her head moved from one end of the cave to another, and up, her chin lifting, outlined by the light of the glowworms, as she looked to the roof of the cavern, dotted with pulsating lights.

Who moved first, Guy couldn't have said. But Lucia melted into his arms, and they stood, his arm around her, the side of her body tight against him. And, as one moment drifted into another, he swallowed and thought he couldn't ever remember feeling so… complete.

But the moment passed, like all other moments. Ridiculous! He was complete within himself. He didn't want another wife; he didn't *deserve* another wife.

He cleared his throat and moved away from her, and immediately the lights dimmed, as the glowworm larvae reacted to a possible threat and retreated into their nests. She looked at him, surprised.

"We should go," he said, and the lights lowered their intensity once more.

She looked at the lights which had revealed their magic for such a short time. He gripped her hand and they walked along the path, out toward the bright reality of daylight. He wouldn't deviate from the path he'd set himself the day he'd buried Hannah. He'd let her down, and she'd paid the consequences. He dared not risk a repeat.

Outside, in the bright midday sun, Lucia blinked and turned to him with an almost shy smile. "Thank you for sharing that. It was amazing."

"As good as art?"

"Definitely."

"I thought it must be. You had the same look about you that you had when you looked at the paintings."

"And I guess this is your kind of art—living, breathing art."

"You got it. And I think you just got me."

Lucia looked faintly startled, and Guy instantly regretted what he'd said.

"Ignore me. That place always gets to me." He looked at the outside of it. "Shame we won't own it much longer."

Her eyes widened. "No! Really?"

"We've gifted it to the Department of Conservation. It's been deemed a place of national importance." He shrugged. "It's not productive land. Best they have it."

She looked into the dark tunnel, and somehow he guessed what she was feeling. Because he was too. They'd connected in there. With a glimpse of the beauty that lay within but which couldn't be had. A beauty that was extinguished by movement or speech. Ephemeral. Just like love, he'd learned, it was a beauty that couldn't be captured because he was liable to destroy it. No, he had no future with anyone, least of all someone as lovely as Lucia.

"It's a shame," she said turning her back to the cave and looking out across the bright landscape.

"Yes, it is," he said, his eyes firmly on her.

Buy A Place Called Home Now!

ALSO BY DIANA FRASER

The Mackenzies

A Place Called Home

Secrets at Parata Bay

Escape to Shelter Springs

What you See in the Stars

Second Chance at Whisper Creek

Summer at the Lakehouse Café

Lantern Bay

Yours to Give

Yours to Treasure

Yours to Cherish

Yours to Keep

Yours Forever

Yours to Love

Italian Romance

The Italian's Perfect Lover

Seduced by the Italian

The Passionate Italian

An Accidental Christmas

British Billionaires

The Billionaire's Contract Marriage

The Billionaire's Impossible CEO

The Billionaire's Secret Baby

Diamond Sheikhs

At the Sheikh's Command

At the Sheikh's Bidding

At the Sheikh's Pleasure

Secrets of the Sheikhs

The Sheikh's Revenge by Seduction

The Sheikh's Secret Love Child

The Sheikh's Marriage Trap

The Sheikhs of Havilah

The Sheikh's Secret Baby

Bought by the Sheikh

The Sheikh's Forbidden Lover

Surrender to the Sheikh

Taken for the Sheikh's Harem

Desert Kings

Wanted: A Wife for the Sheikh

The Sheikh's Bargain Bride

The Sheikh's Lost Lover

Awakened by the Sheikh

Claimed by the Sheikh

Wanted: A Baby by the Sheikh

ABOUT THE AUTHOR

I write emotional, heartwarming romances with stories which make you turn the pages, and characters who feel real—whether they be sheikhs, British billionaires, medieval knights or everyday people whose lives are usually far from everyday (at least in my books).

I live in beautiful New Zealand, just north of Wellington in a small village by the sea. It's here, in a sunny window seat overlooking the hills and trees, that I write my books.

Wherever you are in the world, welcome to my little corner, where I create worlds where people struggle with life and emotions but are always rewarded with love and happiness in the end. Because that's non negotiable!

Diana